BLOODLINE

BOOK 5 ~ TIN STAR K9 SERIES

JODI BURNETT

SDG PUBLISHING

For my Family. We're bound by blood and love. You mean everything to me.

BLOODLINE

Book 5 ~ Tin Star K9 Series

PROLOGUE

Elgin Payne twisted his arms within the confines of the cold silver shackles, painfully catching his wrist bone on the metal cuff. He shook his hand to move the restrictive bracelet further up onto the meatier part of his forearm and glared at the guard whose eyes hadn't wavered from him for forty-five minutes. *Bastard. What does he think I'm going to do? Where would I go?* Elgin tossed his shoulders back against the green, vinyl bench seat of the converted school bus the Washington State Prison System used for transfers. He and four other inmates were being transported from the state penitentiary in Walla Walla to Seattle, where the guards would lock them up again in the Federal Detention Center, SeaTac.

There was no way out of the federal pen besides doing the time. No early release for good behavior coming to him. He slid his gaze to the guard nearest him, letting his imagination roam. Elgin pictured pinning the man against the seat with the chain of his handcuffs crushing the guard's throat, cutting off his air. Of course, the armed officer would simply pull his weapon and shoot him. So as attractive as the action seemed, it wouldn't work. Not even if the other screw and the bus driver weren't in the picture. But they were.

Elgin shifted his feet in the flimsy orange canvas slip-ons the prison guards assigned him right after his body cavity search. Ankle cuffs squeezed tight against his socks. The next half a decade was going to suck. He couldn't figure out how stealing $2500 was just cause for five years and a ten-thousand-dollar fine. What was fair about that? It was as if the system was making money on his theft. Who was the true thief here? Yeah, he'd held a gun to the bank teller's head, but he hadn't shot anyone—this time. His penalty didn't fit the crime. But he'd had a crap lawyer and a jackass judge.

Rain splattered against the window. Light from the moon split into rivulets and raced down the glass in blurry, uneven tracks. As they drove past the lake, the same moonbeams reflected off the turbulent water beyond the embankment below. Elgin watched as more droplets clung to the window. The gentle drizzle trans-formed into liquid missiles as the storm suddenly opened into full fury. An explosion of thunder vibrated through the night sky seconds before the dark canopy lit up with white neon lightning bolts.

"Whoa," murmured the guard. "That was a close one."

Elgin braced his forearms against his thighs and rested his forehead on the seat in front of him. *Not close enough,* he thought.

The bus slowed and the driver honked his horn with a

lengthy blare of emotion. Elgin looked up and peered through the huge windscreen to see what was agitating the man. A convertible, with the top down, swerved into their lane. Three teens rode in the car. Two girls, along with the boy who drove, were holding beer cans and laughing in the face of the raging storm. Music blared. The girl in the back waved her arms recklessly over her head and then flung them around the boy's neck.

Time slowed from that moment on. Elgin watched the boy take a swig from his beer and, in the same second, swerve across the double yellow centerline. The bus driver swore and jammed his hand once again on the horn, finally giving in to being the chicken in the manic race toward each other. He stood on the brakes and yanked the steering wheel hard to the right, attempting to avoid the oncoming vehicle. He was too late. The convertible BMW slammed into the corner of the bus on the driver's side. Elgin stared in fascination as the three young bodies catapulted out of the convertible and smashed into the windshield of the transport mere seconds before the upended car followed them through the glass, killing the kids and the bus driver instantly.

Elgin's chest slammed against the vinyl-covered metal seat in front of him, his head snapping forward and back like a whip. The bus crashed through the guardrail on the edge of the road and careened down the embankment toward the lake below. Everything was a blur painted in dripping watercolor. Trees snapped and whirred by the window. Elgin braced his shoulder in the corner against the seat and the side of the bus, waiting for the final impact.

A strange euphoria overtook him, and his thoughts became calm and clear. If he believed in such things, he might have said he was having an out-of-body experience. He noticed tree limbs scraping against the windows. He watched the guard who had been eyeing him fly through the air and crumple into the ceiling. When the man fell back down, his neck was canted at an unnatural angle. His open eyes stared at nothing. Screams bounced against the metal sides of the bus as they all tumbled downward toward the black lake. The long, metal body tipped onto its side, and Elgin lay pressed against the window as the vehicle came to a shuddering stop.

For one second, Elgin let his mind wander over his body, checking in with each limb. Other than the sharp pain in his neck and upper back, and some bruises and scrapes, he was okay. He could move all his fingers and toes. For a long moment, there was no sound. Elgin pushed himself up and peeked around the edge of the seat. A few other passengers were testing their own limbs. In sudden clarity, Elgin realized he had only seconds, at best, to use this crash to his advantage. He crawled to the dead guard and unfastened his utility belt. He slid the heavy equipment from the man's mid-section and cinched it around his own waist. Elgin was now armed and had the keys to his freedom.

As fast as he could go without drawing attention to himself, he unlocked the shackles binding his ankles and prepared to run. When he checked again, the single remaining guard was giving CPR to one of the other prisoners. The officer remained occupied, but he wouldn't stay that way for long, and besides, he was blocking the easiest exit through the non-existent windshield. Elgin then spotted the emergency escape hatch on the roof of the bus that was now effectively on the side. He stretched his hands toward the release mechanism, but the guard saw him and yelled for him to stop. Elgin dropped back behind the seat, unholstered the gun at his hip, and gripped the weapon. He sprang to his feet and fired. Of the three shots he released, one caught the screw in the throat. The man clutched at the gushing wound as he flew backward.

Elgin wasted no time as he clambered over the bus seats toward the front window. Other prisoners grabbed at him for a hand up, or help, he didn't know. And he didn't slow down to find out. Freedom was within his grasp, and he raced toward it. He climbed through the shattered glass and jumped to the ground below. Rain drenched his clothing in seconds as he dashed for cover in the surrounding trees. He ran along the edge of the lake, gaining as much distance from the accident site as he could before emergency vehicles and more cops showed up. He couldn't afford to get caught this time, after all, a life sentence *was* a fair penalty for the execution he'd just committed.

The scream of oncoming sirens pierced through the dark, sodden sky.

His useless canvas shoes stuck in the mud, doing little to protect his feet, and his orange jumpsuit held the cold rainwater against his shivering skin. Elgin needed to shed the telltale clothing as soon as possible. But for the time being, he struggled against the saturated cloth. Finally, when he felt he'd put enough distance between himself and the crash site, he slowed to catch his breath and unlock the handcuffs from his wrists. Dropping them into the lake, along with the keys, he set off again.

A mile or so later, he came upon a lakeside campground. In all, there were five tent sites and three campers. Lantern light glowed from inside most of the shelters, but on the edge of the loop sat a darkened pop-up with no car or truck nearby. With any luck, the inhabitants were in town. Keeping to the shadows, Elgin edged around the corner and approached the camper entrance. He knocked first, to be sure no one was in there. When no answer came, he tried the knob and found it locked. But the flimsy door couldn't stop him. It would only slow him down.

Minutes later, he'd busted through and was inside choosing a dry set of clothes and a jacket from the occupant's gym bag. Unfortunately, there were no shoes or boots that fit him, so he kept the lame slip-ons for the time being. He took the gun from the guard's utility belt and slid it into the back waistband of the jeans before supplying himself with a flashlight and snacks. Laughing at his good fortune, Elgin stuffed his pockets full of granola bars. He snagged two bottles of water and, after wadding up his prison garb and stuffing it into a plastic bag, he snuck out into the night. From there, he followed the dark paved road out to the highway and headed toward the lights of the nearby town he figured was probably Kennewick.

Elgin stayed off the main streets as he neared the city. He needed a car and found one that would do in a pinch parked behind a seedy 7-11. He broke through the back door window to gain access and quickly hot-wired his ride. As he drove through downtown, heading north toward Richland, he massaged the ache in his tightening neck muscles and consoled himself with the thought of his wife's terrified expression when he appeared in Almira tomorrow, showing up unexpectedly at his house. *That bitch is going to pay the piper for betraying me to the cops.*

By the time the morning sun had warmed the sky, Elgin arrived in Soap Lake. He ditched the hijacked car in a campground parking lot near the lake. No one would wonder about seeing a strange car there. It was another hour's drive to Almira from Soap Lake, and he'd hitch-hike to his hometown from there. Stolen cars were easy to follow—borrowed rides were not. He walked along the two-lane road, holding his thumb out whenever a car passed him, which was a paltry few. His neck hurt and his shoulders ached. By noon, he was exhausted and hungry, so he sat against a tree at the side of the lane and downed three of the cinnamon flavored snack bars and a bottle of water.

An older model truck with a diesel exhaust problem chugged black smog into the blue-skied day as it rambled up the drive toward him. Elgin stood and, waving, flagged the driver down. A grizzled old man leaned across the seat and peered out the open passenger window at him.

"Car trouble?"

"No, sir." Elgin leaned against the door to speak to the man. "I'm just on a journey around the states. Will you give me a lift?"

The driver chewed on his cheek while he considered the plea. He nodded. "Yeah, I guess. If you don't mind riding in the back." He tilted his head toward the bed of his truck.

The fumes might choke him, but Elgin preferred to ride in the back. The driver would have less opportunity to study his features, and besides, Elgin wasn't in a sociable mood. "Not a problem. 'Preciate it." He bobbed his chin and climbed into the dented and rusty bed of the old pickup. He rode the rest of the way to Almira, enjoying the warmth of the sunshine.

A mile from his house, Elgin slapped the edge of the truck, and the driver pulled over. "This will do. Thanks for the ride!" He hopped down and waved as the aged man drove away, leaving Elgin to his dark plans.

He stood across the dirt road from the small one-bedroom farmhouse that he had shared with his wife before the court convicted him of armed robbery and sent him off to jail. There was no movement, but Rose's car sat parked in the carport on the side. She was home. Heat swirled in his gut and a fit of vengeful anger bubbled up. Rose had to pay for what she did, and he planned to enjoy every ounce of pain he inflicted. Every plea for mercy. Elgin's eyes narrowed to slits as his fury boiled.

After assuring himself that no one would see him, he crossed the street and slid between the carport and the house to the backyard. He let himself through the chain-link gate and hopped onto the back porch, reaching for the screen door. It was unlocked, and he opened it slowly so it wouldn't squeak. He stepped into the kitchen. Two plates sat next to the sink with chunks of uneaten crust and potato chip crumbs. His mind did a double take. *Two plates?*

The thought barely registered before he heard muffled sounds coming from down the hall. From his bedroom. Elgin glanced at the clock on the chipped enamel stove. *1:47 p.m.*

Rose cried out from behind the closed door. "Yes!"

A red haze filtered through Elgin's vision. Rose was not alone. He yanked the prison guard's pistol out of his waistband and crept past the small bathroom toward the room he shared with his wife. A deeper voice moaned, and Elgin's palm grew sweaty. At the threshold, he wiped his hand on his pants before re-gripping the weapon and throwing open the door. The scene before him sent pure, white-hot rage screaming through his veins. Without a thought, he acted.

Elgin leveled the gun at the man's head. Wide, dark eyes held surprise and then fear a split second before the back of his skull exploded, spraying blood, bone, and gray matter onto the bed and wall behind him. Rose gripped the sheet to cover her bare chest and screamed.

Blood surged in a thrumming pulse through Elgin's brain as he swung the weapon toward his betraying slut of a wife.

She held up a hand as though to stop him. "No, Elgin! Please! You don't understand!" Still clutching the bedclothes, she scooted to the edge of the mattress. "What are you doing here?"

Elgin kept the gun pointed at her. She spoke, but her words bounced off his awareness. Fury drowned them out and punishment became his sole focus. Rose would pay for this. She was unfaithful. Probably had been many times. *Bitch!* In two strides, he approached her, cracking

9

the pistol grip across her face. The smooth skin on her cheek split on impact, and she fell back onto the bed. Terror filled her eyes and fed Elgin's revenge with hedonic energy.

He unclasped the leather belt he wore and pulled it from the loops on his jeans. Folding it over, he flailed the double strap against Rose's cream-colored thighs, leaving angry welts wherever he struck. She screamed. She cried. He ate it up. Power coursed through him—cold and brutal. He lunged at her and held her down as he slid the belt around her neck and cinched it. She bucked and pleaded, but she was no match for his hate-filled strength. He yanked the leather tight. Within seconds, the fight abandoned Rose. Her eyes bulged, and her limbs grew still.

Elgin then finished the job the stranger had begun. He might not be the only man his wife had screwed, but he sure as hell would be the last.

When he'd spent his rage, Elgin left the mess in the bedroom and went to find something to eat. He heated a leftover cheesy casserole in the microwave and opened a beer. Carrying his plate with him, he gathered some clothes and packable food. He dug through the back of the bedroom closet for a pair of sturdy leather boots. At least Rose hadn't thrown out any of his shit.

Glancing at the blood-splattered clock on his night-stand, he realized he'd spent far too much time there. His house would be one of the first places the cops looked for him, so he decided to wait until he disappeared to change out of the useless prison sneakers he had on.

He shoved the gear he'd gathered into a backpack.

Then, after snatching his pocketknife from the kitchen, he found Rose's purse and car keys. He closed the door behind him as he left. Driving his wife's blue Honda Accord to the highway, Elgin merged, heading east toward Spokane.

1

Throughout Caitlyn Reed's entire life, whenever she had an emotional struggle or issue, she either worked it out physically, or she took off on a long horseback ride through the mountains surrounding her home in northeastern Wyoming. Riding wasn't an option for her right now though, because her horse, Whiskey, was at her parents' ranch. And the last thing she wanted was to face them before she'd come to terms with the huge boulder that had landed smack in the middle of her world. So instead, she had taken her K9 partner, a Belgian Malinois named Renegade, on a ten-mile run before the sun rose that morning. After which, she pressed herself and Ren through their training obstacle course—repeatedly. They were currently on round five. Caitlyn was slick with sweat and exhausted, but she had yet to rid herself of her consternation. Nor had she come up with any real solutions to her dilemma.

Last night the date with her fiancé, Colt Branson, had started off like a romantic dream, complete with sparkly fairy dust. They had finally agreed to set a solid date for their wedding, and their long, blissful life together stretched out before them.

That was until the ice-water-in-her-face effect of the unexpected appearance of Allison Snow-Lopez and her family outside the café. Caitlyn knew Allison was back in Moose Creek. She also knew that Colt had seen Allison on a few occasions and that she'd attempted to reconnect with him. Colt said he'd tried to avoid Allison, not wanting to dredge up their painful past—his drunken one-nighter with her over ten years ago, at their high school graduation party—that had shattered the young, innocent love blossoming between him and Caitlyn. It had taken almost a decade for her to forgive him and learn to trust him again.

Allison had moved away from Moose Creek that fateful summer, but now she was back. That in itself, was no big deal. Not until last night, when she and Colt ran into the Snow clan on the sidewalk outside the Moose Creek Café. The Snow family that included a ten-year-old boy who looked exactly like Colt did when he was that age.

Caitlyn clipped Renegade's vest to the tactical one she wore. She then pulled them both up the rope climb, using only her burning arms to make the ascent. The pain of exertion numbed her feelings but was incapable of chasing them away. She wasn't mad at Colt. Well, she *was*, but the anger and hurt were misplaced. He had been as shocked as she was.

Now, she had to get the huge lump of sadness pressing against the back of her sternum under control before she talked with Colt. In an instant, her life had permanently changed through no action of her own. Suddenly, there was a little boy to think about. A boy who, if he was Colt's son—of which she had no doubt—would become a part of their lives.

Her thoughts were disjointed, emotional, and sometimes irrational. If she was being honest, she didn't want someone else's kid to be their first child. She wanted their babies to be *theirs*. She pictured Jace, with his hazel eyes that mirrored Colt's, and felt flashes of anger toward him. Those feelings needed to be cleaned up. Of all the people involved, Jace was the most innocent. None of this was his fault.

Caitlyn touched the top of the rope climb and then loosened her grip. She slid down faster than she should have and burned the skin on her palms. Their landing jolted up through her legs, and she bent to ease Renegade to the ground. As soon as she unclipped him, she opened a bottle of water and poured it on her blistered hands. Even still, her volatile emotions remained, refusing to be chased or burned away.

"Come on, Ren. Let's hose you off, then I'm hitting the shower."

Renegade loved the water. He leapt up and tried to bite the stream pouring from the hose. Instead, the flow caught him in the nose, and he tossed his head and sneezed. He spun in circles and attempted to catch the water once again. Normally, his antics made Caitlyn laugh. But not today.

"Renegade, stand still," she grumbled at him. Her dog cocked his head and his ears pointed straight up. His black face held a quizzical expression. Shaking the cool water from his tawny coat, he wagged his tail and barked at her. "I'm sorry, Ren. It's not your fault, but I don't feel like playing today. Let's get you a snack, then it's my turn to wash up."

When her dog was happily chewing on his peanut butter-filled Kong, Caitlyn ran the shower as hot as her skin could stand. Maybe she could scald the turmoil away. Last night, when Colt drove her home, she murmured some lame excuse about being tired, and had left Colt sitting in his Jeep outside her cabin. She hadn't slept, nor had she allowed herself any tears.

Standing in the cascade of steaming water, she finally let the emotion come. Tears flowed in torrents. Now was the time for her ten minutes of self-pity and grief. After this, she would cowgirl up and deal with it. She hadn't seen the train wreck coming, but that wasn't an excuse. Caitlyn let the hot shower dilute her pain and frustration until she was ready to take a deep breath and cope.

She patted her pink skin dry and pulled on jeans and a work shirt. Sundays were normally the day—when she had the day off—that Caitlyn spent at Reed Ranch. But she couldn't face her family right now. Not before she and Colt had a chance to talk everything out. They hadn't discussed much about the bombshell that exploded last night. Instead, Colt dropped her off at home and she had sent him back to his house. They both had plenty to think about before they talked it all through.

When her phone rang, Caitlyn figured it was Colt, but the name McKenzie Torrington flashed across the screen. The pretty face in the photo of Caitlyn's friend and future sister-in-law smiled out at her. Caitlyn sighed and tapped on the green dot. "Hey, Kenze. What's up?"

MCKENZIE WOKE early that morning so she could get a running start on the final details for her wedding. She gazed at the long white gown hanging from the closet door in her small apartment. Warm contentment swirled with champagne bubbles of excitement in her belly. Only three more weeks until the big day.

She and Dylan were ready to get married now, but in deference to his sister Caitlyn, who still mourned the death of her partner and friend, Sam Dillinger, they had opted to delay the ceremony for a few weeks. It wasn't that long ago that Sam was killed in the bombing of a federal judge up in Mammoth, Wyoming. Caitlyn and Sam had been sent there to guard the judge after he'd received some emailed threats. Now, Caitlyn blamed herself for Sam's death. She insisted she should have been the one in the judge's chambers when the grenade went off.

Postponing the wedding ended up being a good decision, not just for Caitlyn's sake, but also because McKenzie's new Belgian Malinois mama was ready to deliver her puppies any day. Her Rottweiler's litter had already been claimed. All except for one rumble-tumble Rottie pup. He was the one they'd selected for Sam's young son, Caleb. Caitlyn had wanted Caleb to have a puppy to help the little boy cope with the loss of his father, and McKenzie had agreed it was a wonderful idea.

McKenzie turned on her Keurig coffee machine, and while she waited for the water to heat, she dialed Caitlyn. "Good morning. I didn't wake you, did I?"

Caitlyn laughed over the line. "It's nine o'clock. I've been up for over four hours."

"Right." McKenzie pressed a Cappuccino pod into the slot and closed the lid. "What are you up to today? Want to have lunch?"

"Can't. Colt's coming over later."

McKenzie let out a quiet sigh. She'd wanted to ask Caitlyn to be her maid of honor in person. "Are you guys spending the day at the ranch?"

"Not today."

"Oh." McKenzie failed at keeping the disappointment out of her tone.

"What's wrong?"

"Nothing, really. I just wanted to talk to you."

"You're talking to me now, so shoot."

It was times like these that highlighted the difference between the two friends. Caitlyn was matter-of-fact and shoot-from-the-hip, direct. McKenzie, on the other hand, had flowerier ideas about life. She had pictured Caitlyn and her giggling over wedding plans and shopping together. Honestly, what had she been thinking? Her friend was not that kind of woman. "I wanted to ask you to be my maid of honor."

"Oh... Wow. Yes! Absolutely. I'd love to, but I know nothing about the rules. What do you need me to do?"

McKenzie smiled and thought, *Of course, you don't. But if I needed a home intruder apprehended or my car fixed...* Aloud, she said, "Well, obviously I want you to stand up with me at the wedding and help me with whatever plans still need to be made. Though your mom is a ton of support in that department."

"Doesn't the maid of honor throw the bachelorette party?"

"Yes, if you want to."

"Of course, I do. Will you make a list of who all you want to come?"

Maybe Caitlyn would be better at this than McKenzie originally thought. "I'll email you a list this afternoon."

"Great. Who's going to be Dylan's best man?"

"I think he wants to ask your brother, Logan. He also wants Colt to stand with him, but I don't know who else I'd ask to balance out the wedding party."

"What about Stephanie? You guys have become friends since you started working together at the café, haven't you?"

"Yeah, that's a good idea. I'll ask her."

"We should definitely invite her and Logan's fiancée, Addison, to the bachelorette party."

"Good thinking. I'd like to get to know Addison better since we're going to be family." McKenzie lifted the warm mug, and breathing in the rich scent, sipped her creamy coffee. She leaned back against the counter. "I have something else I wanted to talk to you about, too."

"What's up?"

"Change of subject entirely, but what would you think about breeding Renegade to Athena, my new Belgian Malinois?"

"Are you serious?"

"Yes, why? Don't you think it's a good idea?"

"Well… you *do* know I got Renegade from a rescue, right? He didn't come with any papers. I don't know what his bloodlines are or even if he's purebred."

"With his appearance, temperament, and conformation, I can almost guarantee he is. It's fairly common that people think they want a Belgian Malinois because they watch videos of how amazing they are. But then they get one, and realize the breed has way too much energy and intelligence to be a lazy family dog, content with lying around. So, they take them to a rescue facility. Besides, Renegade has all the qualities I want to propagate. The AKC should be able to help trace his bloodlines. I mean… they might not be able to tell if he's a purebred just by a DNA test, but maybe they can help us find his lineage. If they can and they're able to run it back three generations, then we're good to go."

"And if they can't? I mean, Renegade is awesome, *obviously*," McKenzie heard the pride vibrate in her friend's voice. "But we don't know about any negative traits in his genetics that don't show up in him but might carry through his genes."

"I agree, but I think the risk is small, and I really would love to breed him with Athena. Seriously, both he and Athena have all the outstanding qualities I want to see in my first litter of Malinois puppies."

"When are you planning on doing this? I mean, Athena is a fantastic Mal, but she hasn't even had her current litter yet. I'm sure you need to give her a break."

McKenzie laughed. "Of course, I do. I'm just dreaming ahead."

"How is Athena? She should deliver any day, right?"

"According to her previous owner's records, yes. And she seems ready, but Dr. Moore said it could be another week. I'm headed over to your parents' ranch in a little bit to check on her. Ember's pups are all claimed except for Caleb's little one. I'd like to have him housebroken before we give him to Caleb. That way Laurie won't have to deal with that on top of everything else." McKenzie thought of her Rottweiler dam and the last little Rottie pup before she asked, "How's Laurie doing, by the way? Have you talked to her?" McKenzie's heart ached for the young widow and her son. Caleb was excited to take his puppy, Bear, home, and McKenzie hoped the addition to their little family would soften some of the sharp, jagged edges of their grief, but she didn't want the puppy to be extra work for Laurie.

"At this point, she's just forcing herself to walk through the long, painful days, one at a time. It's good she has Caleb to care for or she might not get out of bed. I feel sick every time I think about Sam dying in that explosion. I wish—"

"Don't say it, Caitlyn. No one had any control over what happened. It is awful that Sam was killed, but you couldn't have prevented it. And it wouldn't have been better if it were you instead. You know that, right?"

"Yeah, but at least *I* don't have a kid."

"Not yet."

"I better go." Caitlyn always cut the conversation off whenever her grief welled up. McKenzie closed her eyes and waited for her to continue. "We'll talk more about breeding our dogs later. We have plenty of time."

"When do you have to go back to work?" McKenzie

kept her voice light. She scanned her wall calendar. Her wedding was only three weeks away. Everything was happening crazy fast, but Stella, her future mother-in-law, was a planning general and so far, had all the details under control. McKenzie's own mom had lost a battle against breast cancer when McKenzie was only fourteen. She wished her mom could be there with her on her special day, but in her mom's absence, McKenzie was beyond grateful for her future mother-in-law, Stella.

McKenzie couldn't ask her dad to be there either. He had dealt with the loss of his wife by attempting to drown his grief in bourbon. He'd started drinking and never stopped. Now, he moved from one side of the country to the other and was hard to get a hold of. But if she was honest with herself, she'd admit she didn't really want him there. He'd only cause a scene.

Caitlyn's voice broke through McKenzie's thoughts. "I have to drive to Casper tomorrow and I'll be there for the week, but we can talk wedding stuff in the evenings, after I get off."

"Thanks, Caitlyn. Are you sure it won't be too much for you to plan the party while you're working?"

"I'm sure. It's just a couple of phone calls. Where do you want to go? The only place in Moose Creek is the Tipsy Cow, and I doubt you want to celebrate at the local honky-tonk."

"Maybe we could go up to Billings or down to Cheyenne? I'm going to leave the details up to you since you're from this part of the world."

Caitlyn laughed. "Sounds good. I'll think of something."

When they ended the call, McKenzie put her breakfast dishes in the dishwasher, grabbed her purse, and headed out to Reed Ranch. Dylan, she was certain, was already out on the acreage working somewhere, but hopefully, he'd come back to the house for lunch. Until then, she and Stella had a long list of tasks to accomplish before the wedding.

McKenzie pulled to a stop near the backyard gate at the Reeds' house. On her way to the kitchen door, she checked on her dogs in their whelping kennels. Ember, the Rottweiler she'd ended up adopting along with Athena, was snoozing in the morning sun with Bear, her last puppy, who had curled up under her front leg. Their black and sable coats glistened in the warmth. Athena, the very pregnant Malinois, struggled to her feet. Heavy with her pending litter, she ambled over to the fence to receive some love and scratches from McKenzie.

"Good morning, girl. Any day now; I promise." McKenzie filled their bowls with fresh, cool water from the hose before going inside. She opened the kitchen door and called, "Good morning."

Stella didn't hear her over the conversation she was having with her husband, John, in the living room. Her future in-laws sounded upset.

John rarely raised his voice, but this was clearly one of those times. "Why can't I just enjoy my damn retirement, Stella? I've worked hard all my life and now I just want to read and fish. Is that so bad?"

"Of course, not... unless that's *all* you want to do. I've worked hard too; in case you don't remember." Stella's tone rose in exasperation. "Who do you think stood by your side all these years, raising the kids, and stretching every dollar? I'd like to enjoy retirement too, only I want to *live* a little—not act like I'm already dead."

"What the hell does that mean?"

"You wake up, ask me what *I'm* making you for breakfast, and then sit on that couch to watch TV or read all day long. That kind of life might work for you, John Reed, but it won't cut it for me. You get to retire, but you still expect me to do all the things I've always done."

"Make breakfast?"

"Yes! Among other things. And you are perfectly capable of making your own damn breakfast. *You* want to rest and take it easy, but how does *my* life get to change?"

"For God's sake, I'll make my own breakfast from now on if it makes you stop harping at me."

McKenzie stood on the other side of the swinging door that led to the main room. She didn't mean to eavesdrop on their argument, but she didn't want to interrupt them either. She bought some time by pouring herself a cup of coffee.

"Harping?" Stella slammed something down. "Are you purposefully not understanding what I'm trying to say? Let me spell it out. I am not content to waste my remaining years becoming part of the sofa. I want to live. I want to travel and have some adventures. I have dreams and I refuse to fade away like the sun-bleached curtain fabric. And I don't see myself waiting on you, hand and foot, for the rest of my life while you get to relax. I'm going to *live* my life with or without you!"

Heavy footfalls marched across the floor in the other room until a distant door slammed. McKenzie took a long sip before she bolstered her gumption and went through into the log home's great room. John stood next to the massive stone fireplace, bracing one arm against the mantle.

"Good morning," McKenzie ventured.

John's head snapped up, and he regarded her with deep brown eyes; the same burnt umber tint all his children had inherited. "McKenzie. I didn't hear you come in."

"Sorry." McKenzie took another drink of coffee, mostly to hide behind her mug. Those eyes pierced her skin.

His voice rumbled low and resigned. "I suppose you heard me and Stella hollering at each other. Sorry about that."

McKenzie shook her head. "Don't be. Every couple argues sometimes."

"That may be, but..." He crossed his arms and, cocking his head, he narrowed his eyes at her. "What's *your* opinion? Do you think all I do is sit around waiting to die?"

"John, I don't want to get in the middle of—"

"Don't you think I've earned the right to spend my days fishing and relaxing?" His ire rekindled. "What about when Dylan retires? Are you going to let *him* enjoy some much-deserved rest?"

Stella returned to the room from down the hall. "I can't believe you're trying to drag McKenzie into this, John. Listen, I'm not going to try to change your mind. I won't stand in your way of sitting around and doing nothing, either. You do whatever you want. But when you can't find me, assume I've hopped on a plane and am having a wonderful time seeing the world somewhere without you!" Her bright blue eyes flashed with anger. "Come on, McKenzie. We have centerpieces to work on." Stella turned on her heel and stomped back toward the office.

If McKenzie could dissolve into the wood flooring, she would. If only Dylan would decide to come home for something—anything—it would save her from feeling so awkward. She was a part of the family now, but that didn't mean it was comfortable stepping into the center of her in-laws' personal struggles. They'd always seemed so solid. Always on the exact same page. She'd witnessed a little tension when John had been sick last winter and refused to go to the doctor, but he had aimed his stubbornness at everyone, not just Stella. And once Blake Kennedy, the town's doctor, had diagnosed John with diabetes, he got on an insulin routine, changed his diet, and everything calmed back down. Other than that, she'd never heard John raise his voice to Stella. Ever.

2

_____

Caitlyn sat across her dining table from Colt. They'd made a pretense of eating dinner, but neither of them had much of an appetite, and the food tasted like sawdust. The sun had long since set and now the only light in the room came from the flickering fire in the hearth. They hadn't broached the touchy subject yet, but the fact that Colt likely had a ten-year-old son he had never been told about, seemed like a tangible object wedged between them. Caitlyn knew Colt was clinging to the hope that the whole thing was a mistake, but when she saw the boy, Caitlyn recognized Colt both in Jace's face and his mannerisms. Jace looked exactly like Colt did when he was a kid running wild on the ranch with her and her brothers. She didn't need a test to tell her that Jace was Colt's son. What she needed was a dose of wisdom on how to deal with the huge earthquake that had suddenly rocked their world. She could only guess at the extent of what the aftershocks were going to cause in their lives from here on out.

For now, no matter how she felt about Jace or the boy's mother, Caitlyn wanted to support and comfort Colt. He'd made one stupid mistake as a high school kid, which had caused pain and trust issues between them for years. Now that they had worked through all of that, and were finally ready to get married, his teenage indiscretion reared up again. It hurt, to be sure, and she hadn't processed all the implications of the situation and how it would affect their lives going forward. She stiff-armed any thoughts about Colt having a child that wasn't hers. She'd think about all of that later when she had more time to herself.

Caitlyn reached across and took Colt's hand. He glanced up from the table, and her heart ached for the pain swimming in his hazel eyes. "Everything will work out, Colt. You'll see."

"I don't even know how to feel. If Jace is mine, then I'm pissed that I never knew about him. It's not fair. Not to me or to the kid. If he's not mine, well... am I a complete ass to hope he's not?" He scrunched his eyes closed and covered them with his free hand.

"Right now, I think you should allow yourself to feel however you feel. Don't force yourself to feel the right way. Who even knows what that is?"

Colt peered at her from under light-brown lashes. "How are *you* feeling? I can't bear to think about how painful this is for you."

Caitlyn shook her head. "I don't know. I think my feelings are secondary right now. I guess I need to sort through it all, but no matter what, Colt, I want you to know you have my love and support. We'll get through this." She stopped short of saying they'd get through it together because what she really wanted—what she needed—was some space to herself to think.

"I'm going to ask Allison to meet with me tomorrow. Will you come too? I want you to be a part of any decisions I make."

Caitlyn rolled her lower lip between her teeth and bit down before she answered. "I think you and Allison need to talk about this with no one else present. We all need some time, but what happens next is up to the two of you."

"You and I are going to be married, Catie. I don't want to make any huge life decisions without your input." He raised his head to look at her, and his eyes deepened their focus. "We're still getting married, right? I mean—"

Caitlyn gripped his hand between both of hers. "Of course, Colt, and I appreciate you wanting to involve me, but it really isn't my place. And I'm sorry, but I'd rather not be there. You have my complete support, and we'll work through whatever you decide. The thing is… none of this is up to me." Her emotions were flexing and getting harder to keep at bay. At the moment, all she needed was to be alone so she could continue to sort through her feelings. The last thing on earth she wanted was to face Allison over a table at the café while they all pretended to sip a friendly cup of coffee and discuss how their lives were all about to change forever.

Caitlyn brought Colt's hand to her mouth and kissed his rough knuckles. "Listen, why don't we both get some sleep? Things will look clearer in the morning. They always do." Colt stood and pulled Caitlyn to her feet and embraced her. She pressed her cheek against his chest and held tight, breathing in the fresh cedar scent of his after-shave. Her phone vibrated in her back pocket. "I better get that." She glanced at the back-lit screen. "It's my chief." Caitlyn stepped away from Colt and answered.

"Sorry to call so late, Reed, but there was a prisoner escape up in Washington last night. It happened during a prison transfer when the bus went off the road. One of the men, an Elgin Payne, in for five years on an armed robbery conviction, escaped. When the police went to his home to interview his wife, they found her, and another man murdered in the bedroom. Her car is missing, so the current assumption is that Payne came home, found his wife with another man, killed them both, and ran. He's a fugitive now, and as such, falls under the US Marshals' purview."

"Okay. And you're calling because you want me to take Renegade out there to see if we can track him?"

"Exactly. Marshals in Washington followed his move-ment to Spokane because he was stupid enough to use his wife's credit card for gas, but I don't expect him to continue down that path of stupidity. If he ditches the car, we'll need to track him on the ground if we can."

"I understand. So, should I report to Spokane?"

"Yes. How soon can you get there?"

"I'm guessing it is about a twelve- or thirteen-hour drive from here. If it's okay, I'd like to have my own vehicle out there rather than fly in and have to rent some-thing. I could be there by dinnertime tomorrow."

"That works for me. Call me when you get there."

"Will do." Caitlyn ended the call.

Colt had been listening, and when she met his gaze he asked, "Gotta go on a case?"

"Yeah. There was a prison bus accident and one of the convicts escaped. The Marshals want Renegade on scene in the hope he can track the guy on the ground." Caitlyn shifted her gaze away from Colt's penetrating stare. She didn't want him to read the relief in her eyes that she felt at having an excuse to leave town for a few days. It would be better for them both if she had some time and space to deal with her own confused feelings, and to get the DNA test results back before she had to face her family with the news. She needed to let herself feel her emotions without the pressure of behaving the right way. "I should pack. Ren and I need to head out first thing."

COLT SENSED Caitlyn's inner shift from being totally present with him to her more detached work mode. She was already compartmentalizing her mind on the new case. He stuffed his hands in his pants pockets. "I should probably head home since you have an early morning and need to pack."

She hesitated. "I'm sorry. Do you mind? I mean... do you still want to talk?"

He wanted to talk, and he wanted to take her to bed. He wanted to lose himself in her and ignore the shocking realities that were crashing into his life. "No, it's okay. Call me tomorrow night when you get settled in Spokane. I'll have talked to Allison by then and have a better idea of where all of this is going."

"I'd rather you call me right after you're done speaking with Allison. I'll just be driving. We can talk then." She set her phone on the table and slid her arms around his waist. "We'll get through this—whatever ends up happening. We're in this together." She stretched up on her toes to kiss him.

The warmth of her lips drew him in, and he held her close, not wanting to let go. He buried his nose in her coconut-scented hair, wishing they could rewind the past twenty-four hours and not go out for ice cream. If only they'd stayed at the restaurant for dessert—ordered the crème brûlée—they wouldn't have run into Allison. Of course, that was an irrational thought. Jace would still be in the picture, whether they saw him or not, and Catie would still be leaving town to go to work.

Colt cupped Caitlyn's soft cheek in his hand, and she pressed into it. "Thanks for being so supportive, Catie. I know this is a huge shock. It certainly is for me. We both need some time to figure out how this will change things." He kissed her forehead and then, releasing her, he lifted his hat from the table and turned toward the door. "I'll talk to you tomorrow. Drive safe and be vigilant."

Caitlyn slipped a finger through his back belt loop and followed him out onto the porch. "I will. Always am."

He crouched down and stroked Renegade's black face. "You too, buddy." The dog swiped Colt's chin with his pink tongue. Colt chuckled and wiped his face on his sleeve before he kissed Caitlyn a final time.

. . .

WHEN COLT GOT HOME, he grabbed a beer from the fridge and sat in front of his laptop. Before he talked to Allison and insisted on a DNA test, Colt wanted to know what his rights were if, in fact, Jace belonged to him. He scanned through several legal sites and was struck by a heavy reality. If he was a father, he had the full rights and responsibilities of a parent. Obviously, he had a financial responsibility, but he wondered if that would be retroactive or start now since he hadn't known before. If Jace was his son, he wanted to provide for him, not just with money, but as a father should. He wanted to know the boy and help raise him. Did he have visitation or custody rights?

The thing was, he didn't want Allison in his life. At all. Colt chugged his malty beer. He had no real choice in the matter, though, not if Jace was his. The son came with his mother. Colt's thoughts and feelings were all over the map. The whole situation was a mess, but somewhere deep inside, a warm ember glowed with the idea that he might have a son. As soon as the thought surfaced, guilt flooded over him. None of this was fair to Caitlyn. She didn't want this. There was no positive in this mess for her. *Christ. What am I gonna do?*

Colt closed his computer and turned on the TV. Sleep would not come easy, but maybe he could distract himself until it did. He found the remote and switched over to the sports channel. A replay of the Masters Tournament in Augusta, Georgia, filled the screen. Colt wasn't into golf, but he left the broadcast on anyway and sat on the couch. A file folder laying on the coffee table caught his eye. He'd printed the name "Burroughs" in all caps across the front.

Colt reached for the report and scanned the details on the first page. Raymond Burroughs: Bank Robber, Jewelry Thief, Drug Dealer, and Murderer. The man showed up in the mountains above Moose Creek last February and proceeded to destroy the Woodrow family. Ray Burroughs and Woodrow's wife, Elaine, ran off together, but not before Burroughs and his gang killed her husband and son, and kidnapped her daughter. Caitlyn, as part of a team of US Marshals, along with an ATF unit, rescued the girl, but Burroughs had escaped with Elaine.

A month ago, Colt discovered Burroughs at a meth lab up in Montana. But when bullets started flying, the lab blew up, and the slippery bastard snuck away amid the chaos once again. Burroughs caused nothing but death and destruction, and Colt was determined to hunt him down. Starting at the front of the file, Colt re-read every word, letting his mind sift through the details. He itched to catch Ray Burroughs and send him to prison, where he could no longer ruin innocent people's lives.

ELGIN SET the cruise control at two miles an hour over the limit. He didn't want to draw any attention to himself for either going too fast or too slow. The gas gauge hovered a few fumes above empty. His wife was such a stupid bitch. She never could remember to fill her tank. Rose's inability to do the simplest things had been the topic of many of their arguments. She always said she was going to do it tomorrow, or she forgot, or one of a million other brain-less excuses. Why could the woman never do as she was told? Anger ignited in his chest, but it was pointless. He couldn't punish her for her thoughtlessness anymore.

The muscles in his legs and arms tightened and his arms twitched. Elgin gripped the steering wheel as hard as he could, bracing against the familiar sensation. *Damn it!*

Once he arrived in Spokane, he pulled off the road and found the nearest gas station. He could use some smokes, but he didn't dare go inside and show his face on the security cameras. With a wave of nostalgia, he remembered the days when he could still remove his car's license plates, fill her up, and then race away without paying. But that scheme didn't work anymore, now that you had to pay at the pump, and he had no cash. He'd have to use the credit card in his wife's purse. The cops would track him to this location as soon as he inserted it, but what choice did he have? He'd have to outsmart them.

3

C olt poured himself a second cup of bitter coffee. He hadn't slept well after tossing and turning most of the night, and finally got up before dawn and went into the Sheriff's Office early. His eyes itched, and he was in a dismal mood. The acid in the coffee served to burn his stomach rather than settle it. The fact that he might have a ten-year-old son was a curve ball he didn't see coming. His stomach ached like he'd been hit in the gut with one of All-Star, Corbin Burnes', 98 mile-per-hour fastballs.

Caitlyn had said all the right things last night, and he knew she would stand by him, no matter what, but still, she had shrunk back from the situation emotionally. She'd seemed relieved when she got a work assignment that took her out of state. Not that Colt could blame her. He was damn lucky she didn't just tell him to go to hell.

This was his rodeo to deal with, and that's exactly what he planned to do. He scrolled through his phone until he found the voice message that Allison had left him several weeks ago, asking to talk to him. He'd never responded to her, wanting to avoid any conflict with Caitlyn. Now, he realized, he probably should have called her back. Maybe she had wanted to tell him about Jace then, and he could have softened the blow to Caitlyn. Seeing Allison and her son together the other night had been a huge shock for him and Caitlyn. It was immediately apparent to them both that Jace appeared to be a mini version of Colt.

He swallowed against the acid in his belly and tapped the call-back button on his phone.

"Hello?" Allison's smooth voice floated over the line.

"Allison? This is Colt."

"Yes... Colt. I was wondering when I'd hear from you. I thought you might call yesterday."

He noticed she'd said, *when*—not *if*. That pretty much told him all he needed to know. "Do you have something you need to tell me? Something you should have told me ten years ago?" Anger boiled up his throat.

"Colt..." She paused. "Can we meet for coffee or something? I'd rather talk to you in person."

"Yeah. In fact, that's why I called. Do you want to meet at the café?"

"I'm at my parents' tire shop. I can meet you at the café at ten."

"I'll be there." He clicked off and, running a hand down over his face, flopped into his chair.

The whole situation sucked. Well, almost the whole thing. Deep down, under the stress and potential upheaval, was a tiny glimmering thought. *I might have a son.* Whenever the thought passed through his mind, Colt pushed it away, guilt and shame replacing it. First, here he was, putting Caitlyn through more undeserved crap, and second, even though he hadn't known about the boy, he'd effectively been a dead-beat dad. That image led to an explosion of fury aimed at Allison. If Jace was his son, she had no right not to tell him.

Colt had to get off the emotional rollercoaster. At least until he knew the truth for sure. The up and down of it all made him queasy. He'd know for certain soon; he needed to be patient.

His deputy, Wes Cooper, entered through the front door whistling to himself. "Mornin'," he said as he hooked his deputy hat on the rack. "You're here early."

"Yeah, but I've got a meeting at ten. While I'm out, I want you to keep searching for any trace of Raymond Burroughs. He can't have disappeared into thin air. Any luck with finding his relatives in the Dakotas?"

"Not yet, but I'll get on it right away." Wes poured himself a cup of coffee and turned on his laptop.

Colt attempted to work, but his focus was shot. "I'm gonna to get out of here. I'll be back after lunch." Wes nodded and Colt left the office.

He drove up to Moose Lake and parked in the empty lot facing the mountain reservoir. To ease his growing agitation, he got out of his Jeep and walked to the edge of the water. The fresh, pine-scented air soothed his mood. He skipped stones across the lake's glass-smooth surface. The visual metaphor of stones disrupting the still water and creating far-reaching ripples was not lost on him. He agonized over the impact a surprise son might have on his and Caitlyn's relationship and their future, but he also feared what her dad would think of him. John would have no doubt of Colt's betrayal of Caitlyn in high school, and the man Colt admired most would be ashamed of his lack of responsibility toward the boy and Allison.

John was like a father to Colt, but in the end, Caitlyn was John's baby girl. The man would be angry, and worse, disappointed. Dylan would probably punch Colt in the face, but Caitlyn's big brother had little to say if he compared this situation to his own past behavior with women. Her middle brother, Logan, on the other hand, was as solid as they came. Colt's childhood friend was a man of integrity and honor. His disappointment would sting as much as his father's. Colt threw one last stone with all his might before he returned to his Jeep and drove to the café.

Allison was already there when he entered. Her perfectly styled, pale-gold hair shifted when she waved a manicured hand, but she didn't smile. Colt slid into the booth across from her. Stephanie, the café manager, had followed him and set two mugs down on the table.

"You two want breakfast?" she asked as she poured coffee from a silver-bottomed glass carafe.

Colt shook his head. "None for me—Allison?"

"No. Coffee will be fine. Thank you." She kept her gaze fixed on the table.

Stephanie shrugged. "Okay, let me know if you change your minds." She lingered. "Is Caitlyn meeting you?"

If Colt wasn't so tense, he'd laugh at the woman's attempt to pry. "No. She's working."

"Hmm. Well, just give me a holler if you need

anything." Stephanie shifted narrowed eyes to Allison before she finally left them alone.

"So," Colt started. "I'll ask you again. Do you have something you need to tell me? I mean, I couldn't help noticing an obvious resemblance between your son, and me."

Allison picked at an invisible crumb on the table with her long, red fingernails. "All I really want to say is that I might have had something to tell you when I came to town. But since you're engaged to Caitlyn Reed now, and clearly have no intention of changing that, I've decided *not* to accept my parents' job offer to take over their business here in Moose Creek. I'm going to go back to Missouri to look for work there."

"What?" Colt bolted forward, bracing his arms against the table. "What about Jace? And how does my being engaged to Catie have anything to do with you?"

"It's better this way, Colt." She ran her finger around the rim of her cup.

"Better for who?" His pulse sped up. Desperation gripped his chest, and a sense of injustice overcame him.

"Better for everyone. Certainly, better for *you*, and in the end, better for me… and most importantly, it's what is best for Jace."

Colt pinned her to the booth with his intensity. "Allison, is Jace my son?" She looked away but didn't answer. "I want to have a DNA test done. Then we'll know. We'll all know for sure."

Gradually, Allison swung her gaze back to him. "Listen to me. I want what's best for Jace, and that is what I'm going to do."

He realized his fervency was backing Allison into a defensive position, so Colt forced himself to relax. "Of course, you want the best thing for your son. Don't you think that includes having a man in his life? A father?"

"He does." Her gaze dropped to the table. "Or he did, anyway. About two years ago now, my husband, Jace's dad, lost his life in a horrible traffic accident on his way to work."

Her story stunned Colt. "I'm sorry," he murmured. Was it possible that Allison's dead husband *was* Jace's dad?

"And Jace has my father, too. So, he'll be fine."

"Allison, you haven't answered my question. Is Jace mine?" He stretched his hand across the table and gripped her forearm. "You can't deny how much he looks like me."

She stared at his hand. "Ed is the only dad Jace has ever known. Can't we just let sleeping dogs lie?" She glanced up at him with unshed tears flashing in her eyes.

"Damn it, Allison." He pulled his hand back and sat against the booth. "All this time. You should have told me. It's not fair. I should have known—should have had the opportunity to do the right thing."

"And what would have been the right thing, Colt? Would you have married me?" She glared at him. "Don't be ridiculous. Besides, the truth is, I wasn't sure if you *were* the father, or if it was Cody. You and I, well, we only happened that one time. I'd been dating Cody most of senior year, remember?"

"Cody has black hair." Colt's gut twisted and gurgled.

"Yes, Colt, but I didn't know what my baby would look like when I found out I was pregnant. I left town and went to live with my aunt in Missouri. That's where I met Ed

Lopez. We fell in love, and he asked me to marry him. Everyone assumed Jace was his, and we let them. Ed was a wonderful father to my son."

"I still had a right to know."

"What difference would it have made? Don't you see, it was better this way? Jace had a father. He had legitimacy. You had your freedom and… Caitlyn."

"I had a son. Damn it, Allison! I would have helped you. I could have known him."

"You're only thinking of yourself. I had to think of Jace, and Ed too. He was so good to us. It was—"

"It was the easy way out." Colt pushed his coffee mug away. "I want a DNA test done, and if it proves that Jace is mine, which we both know it will, then I have rights." He swallowed back his rising anger. His tone was sharp, he knew, but it was hard to be kind when he hadn't sorted through all his thoughts and emotions.

"Rights? What do you want, Colt? Can't you just leave this alone?"

"No. I can't. I won't."

"How does Caitlyn feel about all this? I can't imagine she'd be happy to know you're pushing for parental rights for a child you don't even know."

"Not that it's any of your business, but Caitlyn supports me whatever happens."

Allison sighed and leaned toward him. "We must do what is right for Jace. Ed is the only father he's ever known. Why would you disrupt that?"

"What about money? I have an obligation to help care for him—to provide for him. And now that Ed is gone, the boy needs a father."

Allison sat back against the booth and crossed her arms over her chest. "Maybe I'll get remarried someday."

"Is that it? Is that what your behavior at the Tipsy Cow was all about? Were you hoping something would start up between us when you came home?" The memory of Allison dressed in her citified mini dress, draping herself all over him at the local bar flashed through his mind.

She shrugged one shoulder. "I'd heard you were still single. I guess I let myself hope…"

Colt clenched his jaw. "Jace is a replica of me at that age. How exactly did you think this was all going to play out? If all went according to your plan, were you *ever* going to tell me about Jace on your own? Or were you hoping to let me believe he was another man's son?" He shook his head in disgust.

She studied him without responding for several minutes. "Regardless, I'm taking my son back to our home in Missouri. That's it. I want nothing from you."

"Well, that's *not* all there is to it. I have rights, Allison, and I intend to claim them. Now, are you going to cooperate? Or do I have to get a court order?"

Allison's voice rose an octave. "Are you serious? Why can't you just leave this alone?"

"A couple of reasons. First, as a man, I have a duty and obligation to my son. Second, Jace needs a father. My dad died when I was his age, and it was hard growing up without him. If it hadn't been for John Reed, I don't know how I would have turned out." Allison glared at him, and he softened his tone. "Look, I don't want to hurt you or make things difficult. I want to help. But I also want to get to know my son. *That's* what I believe is the right thing to do."

A single tear finally escaped over her lower lid and tracked down her cheek. "Jace will hate me."

"No, he won't." Colt took her hand. "He'll see that you were only trying to do what was best for him. He might be angry and confused at first, but he'll eventually understand. And he'll be a better man for knowing the truth. He'll see how you were trying to protect him, and that you told him the truth when he was old enough to hear it."

Allison sighed. "Can I think about it?"

"There's not much to think about. I'm not giving you a choice."

She squeezed her eyes closed and nodded slightly. "Underneath, I suppose I knew it would come to this one day. How do we do the test?"

4

Caitlyn took Renegade on a long early-morning run before she packed up and hit the highway. It was almost 6 a.m. by the time they drove through Gillette on their way up to Billings and she wondered if Colt was up yet. This was going to be a hell of a day with only highway driving to distract her from what was going on back in Moose Creek.

By the time they drove into Billings, it was time to stop for a break. Caitlyn went to the McDonald's drive-thru for a quick breakfast and some hot coffee. The smell of the deep-fried hash brown patty in the paper bag the cashier handed her made her mouth water. She took her egg and cheese biscuit meal to a dog park she found through Google, and let Renegade stretch his antsy legs. It was 10:12 a.m. when she checked her phone. Colt was meeting with Allison at that very minute. A green sticky sensation clogged her throat, and she mentally chastised herself. There was no reason to feel jealous or threatened. Colt had no interest in Allison. But it still stuck in Caitlyn's craw that the woman would likely be a permanent fixture in their lives from now on.

Renegade made friends with a German Shepherd—the only other dog in the park—and Caitlyn nodded politely at the man who brought him. She chewed through her greasy sandwich and washed it down with orange juice and surprisingly good coffee. After tossing a stick a few times for the dogs to chase, Caitlyn was eager to get back on the road.

"Come on, Ren. Time to load up." She opened her truck door, and Renegade sprang inside, still full of energy. She smirked at him as she made her way to the driver's side. Sliding in next to her dog, she shoved him over to his side of the bench seat. He wagged his tail and barked at her. "I hope you're planning on taking a nap at some point, crazy dog." She clipped her belt. "I wish I had *your* energy."

Renegade sat sideways on the bench facing her, his long pink tongue lolling out the side of his mouth over his sharp teeth. He slurped some drool and panted some more before he yipped.

Caitlyn laughed. "I'm going, I'm going!" She tossed her arm around him and squeezed him tight, finding comfort in his steadfast love and loyalty. "What would I ever do without you, Ren?"

By the time they left the outskirts of Billings, he had relaxed and laid down on the seat. Caitlyn's eyes wandered to the digital clock on the dashboard. 11:11 a.m. When she was a kid, she'd believed it was lucky if you caught the clock at 11:11 and she'd make a wish. In honor of her childhood self, she silently wished that Colt would call and tell her everything had been a silly mistake. That Jace wasn't his, and that Allison was leaving Moose Creek forever. It wasn't too much to hope for... was it?

Caitlyn stopped for lunch in Butte, Montana. It was almost 2:30 p.m. by then, and Colt still hadn't phoned. She didn't want to call him in fear of interrupting something. Maybe he and Allison were at the clinic right then having the blood tests done. Surely, he'd call soon.

Inwardly, she rolled her eyes at her morning's wish that Jace wasn't Colt's son. She had no real doubt that the boy was his. She grew up looking at that same face. But since Colt hadn't called with any information, she worried about him.

During their lunch break, Caitlyn put Renegade through some training exercises. She hid his toy and threw her keys out into the middle of a field and told him to find them both. She'd never find the bottom of his energy, but she could tire out his brain enough to keep him from bouncing all over the cab. It had been a long drive so far, and they still had another four and a half hours to go.

They were passing through Missoula when her phone rang. She snatched it up, hoping to see Colt's photo on her screen. But it wasn't him. It was an unknown Washington number—no doubt her temporary duty station. "Reed, here."

"Deputy Reed, this is Chief Styles in Spokane. How far out are you?"

"I've got a little over two hours to go. I'll call you when I get to Coeur d'Alene."

"Sounds good. The team will still be here when you

arrive. We'll be working around the clock till we bag this guy."

"I'll hurry."

"See you soon."

Caitlyn's brain shifted compartments. She considered all they knew about Elgin Payne, and everything he'd done after his escape from the bus crash. His first instinct was to go home. *Did he think his wife would be happy to see him? Or did he know she was sleeping with someone else?*

Caitlyn passed through Coeur d'Alene. She only had thirty-three miles to go before she was in Spokane. She lifted her phone from the drink carrier and called the Spokane Marshals Office. After speaking to the receptionist, she was patched through to the chief.

"Deputy Reed, I want to confirm that you brought your dog with you."

"Yes, of course, sir." Caitlyn glanced down at the napping K9 sprawled out on his back across two-thirds of the truck's bench seat.

"I sure appreciate it. This is a dark case and I want this guy apprehended yesterday. We'll fill you in on all the details as soon as you get here. Have you had dinner?"

"No, but I should be in Spokane in about thirty minutes, or so."

"Grab some food to-go and bring it with you when you get here. It'll be a working dinner."

"Will do."

When she pulled off the highway, she passed a McDonald's. Contrary to popular belief, you *could* have too much McDonald's, so she settled on Taco Bell. Dinner of champions. It wasn't the healthiest choice, but she loved their Gorditas. In the drive-through, Caitlyn ordered a bag full of tacos along with her meal. It was always a good idea to feed the natives.

Renegade whined when he smelled the food. "Sorry, boy. But I don't even *want* to know what this would do to your digestive track." She scratched his head and ears. "But don't worry. I'll let you out to run a little and feed you before we go inside." Her Belgian spun in circles on the seat next to her. The dog needed to burn off some of the high-octane juice zipping through his veins. He'd been sitting in the car for far too long.

Renegade gobbled down a bowl of kibble, then ran from tree to tree on the small green lawn in front of the Marshals building. He did his best to mark every possible tree trunk, shrub, and post in the area. After he calmed down, Caitlyn clipped a short leash onto the back of his US Marshal K9 vest and went inside to meet her temporary work team.

A group of five men and one woman nodded to her when she approached, but they applauded when they realized she'd brought them tacos. "Brownie points, for sure." A heavily muscled man with a crew cut rose to shake Caitlyn's hand. He stood a good two inches shorter than her. "Tim Sands. Glad to have you here, Reed."

One of the female marshals reached into the bag and snagged a taco. "Well, taco points anyway. And I think those are worth more than brownies." Red-tinged oil from the wrapper ran down the dark skin of her hand, and she swiped it up with a long lick. After rubbing her arm on the leg of her jeans, she held out her hand. "Mara Gold." Caitlyn shook Mara's hand, and then the woman squatted down. "This must be Renegade. We've heard a lot about you." She peered up with almost black eyes. "Can I pet him?"

Caitlyn smiled. "Yeah. And thanks for asking. Most police and military K9s aren't dogs you should pet without checking with their handler, but I raised Renegade in my family's home, so he's pretty social. Be careful though, he's had his eye on those tacos since I got them, so watch yours or he might go for it."

Mara set her food in the center of a nearby desk and returned to make friends with Renegade. He licked her fingers before she could stroke his head. "You still smell that spicy beef, don't you?"

An easy camaraderie settled among the group of deputies while they ate tacos and tossed jokes back and forth. Before long, the Chief Deputy Marshal came out of his office to join the fray. "Welcome to our humble abode, Reed. I'm Mark Styles." He shook her hand.

"Chief. Glad to meet you. I'm happy to help."

"I hope you mongrels saved me one of those tacos." He pulled the last taco from the greasy bag with a happy sigh. "Has anyone updated Reed on the situation?" Heads shook. "Okay, well, you know we're chasing escaped convict, Elgin Payne, who, since his disappearance, has allegedly murdered three people, including one of his guards, and he's stolen a car."

"Who else did he kill besides the guard?" Caitlyn asked.

"His wife, and the man she was in bed with when Payne got home."

Caitlyn cocked her head in thought. "Are we sure it was Payne who killed them?"

"A FedEx driver called the police when he approached the door with a delivery, and saw bloody sneaker prints on the porch. He knocked on the door and called out, but when no one answered, the driver opened the door and stepped inside. He saw the wife's body from the entryway and called 911. The shoe prints matched the type of shoes convicts wear in prison. Investigators at the murder scene have discovered that Mrs. Payne was strangled to death. They found her with a belt tightened around her neck. She was beaten and raped before she was strangled. They also found a dead man in the room. He died from a gunshot wound to the head. Semen was detected on the wife's body, but we're still waiting for the lab results on that. The investigator's best guess is that Payne came home and surprised his wife with her lover. In a jealous rage, he allegedly shot the guy and then raped and strangled his wife."

Unable to break fully away from her investigative mind, Caitlyn said, "I know it's highly probable that Payne is the killer, Chief, but shouldn't we wait to see if the lab confirms it was him?"

"That's for the cops and the trial lawyers. For the purposes of the US Marshals, it doesn't really matter. Payne is an escaped convict and a federal fugitive. That's all we need to know to hunt him down."

"I get that, but we don't want to go on a wild goose chase based purely on assumptions."

"That's true, Reed." Chief Styles gave her half a grin. "But this is all we have to go on right now, and I don't want to waste time waiting on the lab. It's too much of a coincidence that his wife was murdered less than twenty-four hours after he escaped. Either way, the killer stole Payne's wife's car and drove to Spokane. We know he came here because, like the stupid criminal he is, he used her credit card to buy gas."

Mara added, "There's a video recording of the man at the gas station. It only captures his back, but we have an image of the clothes he was wearing at that time, which was 1:30 a.m. this morning. He kept his face turned away, so we still don't have a positive ID."

Caitlyn turned to Renegade. She flattened her hand and motioned toward the floor, giving him the silent signal to lie down. He immediately obeyed, and continued to watch her every move. She perched on the corner of someone's desk, and said, "That was over seventeen hours ago. Do we have any indication of which direction he went when he left the gas station?"

Gold turned her desktop monitor toward the group. "Let's watch the video again." She typed in a URL and opened the video file.

Styles pointed at the screen with the tip of his ball-point pen. "This particular convenience store is right off the interstate, and as you pointed out, Reed, he's had seventeen hours to hunker down somewhere or travel in any direction. Whoever the man in the video is, he was careful to keep his face away from the camera angle."

As the footage continued, a second car, a dark-colored Jeep Gladiator, pulled up on the opposite side of the pump, and a short man with glasses slid out. Caitlyn squinted her eyes to focus on the details. "Look. That guy just said something to our suspect. Do we have his license plate number? If we can find him, he might be able to confirm the suspect's identity."

Sands shook his head. "The video never gives us a clear shot of his license. We have the first three letters, but none of the numbers. Our guys are working on it, though."

Gold crossed the room to a map of the northwestern United States that was mounted on the wall behind a sturdy panel of plexiglass. With a red dry-erase marker, she drew a circle that encompassed a thirty-mile distance around Spokane. "Our unsub is somewhere inside this circle. For now."

Sands approached the map and bent close to study the distance. "Unless he flew somewhere."

Gold studied him with her dark eyes. "He couldn't have flown out of Spokane International because the facial identity at TSA Security would have flagged him. I suppose he could have slipped out of one of the smaller airports, but he would have had to plan that type of escape in advance. He couldn't possibly have known ahead that the bus would crash, and as far as we know, he didn't have any money."

Caitlyn rolled her lower lip between her teeth. "Chief, do we have anything belonging to Payne that I can give Renegade to use as a scent marker to track from?"

"What difference would that make?" asked a deputy leaning against the doorframe. "How can a dog track someone in a car?"

"You're assuming he drove away in that car, but it's possible he knew he was on camera, drove out of the view, and dumped the car. Maybe he stole a different one?" Several of the deputies responded with skeptical brows hitching up their foreheads. "Look, I'm not saying I think that *is* what happened. Just that something like that *could* have happened and Renegade can tell us if it did. Has anyone been to the gas station yet? We won't know what other evidence we might find in that parking lot until we go look. One time, Renegade found a plastic wrapper in a liquor store parking lot that ended up being evidence in a drug crime."

Chief Styles frowned as he listened. "It won't hurt to take your dog over there, I guess, but what else is within the focus area? Have we had any word from the local cops about spotting Mrs. Payne's car anywhere? Has someone checked traffic cameras?" Two deputies left the group for their desks.

Sands, still studying the map, crossed his arms. "One thing I know for sure, the longer we stand around talking about it, the farther away Payne is going to get."

Styles nodded and ordered the team, "Let's, get out there, and find this guy before he kills anybody else."

The office full of deputies moved all at once. Mara popped her chin toward Caitlyn. "You two can ride with me. Unless you have a K9 vehicle, you'd rather drive."

"I wish. I just have my personal truck, so thanks. Ren, *knoze.*" Renegade hopped to his paws and scurried to Caitlyn's left heel. He stared up at her, vibrating with energy as he waited for his next command. When she stepped off, he moved with her toward the door.

Stopping for gas had been a huge risk. Elgin had found a cloth cap in the backseat of Rose's car and tugged it down low over his face. With any luck, no one could identify him from the security cameras he knew had filmed him. His greater concern had been the man who pulled in and stood across from him at the pump. While he filled his tank, the guy had noticed when Elgin spaced out for a minute and asked if he was okay. It was hard for Elgin to pull himself out of the confusion that often fogged his brain, but he had done it. This time.

His first impulse had been to make sure the man couldn't identify him. But shooting someone on a city street would draw far too much attention. When Elgin's gas tank was full, he got into Rose's car and drove it to the edge of the parking lot, hopefully beyond the video camera's range.

"Hey!" he opened the door and called out to the stranger. "Can you help me out a minute?" If he could convince the guy to come over to him, he could make sure he never told anyone anything, ever again.

"What's up?" The man yelled back as he finished gassing his truck and returned the nozzle to the hook. He shut the cover over the Gladiator's tank, climbed in, and pulled away from the pump. Stopping next to the Honda, the man leaned out his window and asked, "Are you okay?"

"I'm not feeling so well..." Elgin sat sideways in the driver's seat with his feet resting on the pavement. He bent over as if his belly hurt.

The man climbed out of the truck and approached Elgin. "Are you going to be sick? Should I call someone?"

Elgin motioned him nearer but didn't say anymore. The last thing he needed was for the idiot to dial 911. The truck blocked any view of them from the road. Just two more steps and he'd be near enough. Elgin gripped the pocketknife he hid in his sweaty hand at the side of his thigh and silently encouraged, *Come on man, just a little closer.*

5

Caitlyn followed Mara out to her dark gray Ford Explorer. "You sure you're good with having my dog ride in your car?"

"Yeah, no problem. It's cool hanging with a K9 team." Mara almost smiled before she clicked her key fob and unlocked the doors. "How come you don't have a K9 vehicle?"

"Good question." Caitlyn dreamed of getting a specially fitted K9-SUV like Logan had for his dog, Gunner. His FBI-K9 vehicle was an Explorer like Mara's, but it was designed with a kennel in the back that gave Gunner room to pace around. His vehicle had automatic internal temperature controls that turned the air conditioning on if it got too hot, and the heat if it got too cold, whether Logan was in the car, or not. The coolest feature was the automatic door-popping mechanism. If Logan was outside the vehicle and needed help while Gunner was still shut inside, Logan could press a button on his utility belt that remotely opened the back door to the kennel and his dog could jump out and come to his aid.

Mara followed Sands and another deputy to the gas station where Mrs. Payne's car was last seen. When they got there, Caitlyn took Renegade with her to the exact spot the man on the video had stood about twenty-four hours ago. The trail was already cold.

Renegade lowered his nose to the ground and sniffed the cement lanes on both sides of the fuel pumps, but without an original scent to track, he couldn't help. While other marshals interviewed the two employees inside, Caitlyn walked Renegade along the perimeter of the property. The store sat on a corner, so streets bordered two sides of the lot. To the rear was a small vacant piece of land, beyond which was a privacy fence guarding the yard of a single-family home. A double fence, with chain-link on one side and tall wooden planks on the other served as a boundary between the convenience store and a run-down strip mall hosting a laundromat, a nail salon, a Pho restaurant, and a liquor store.

Mara and Sands were talking to the owner of the nail place when Renegade paused at the rocky edge, sniffed, and sat down. He barked to get Caitlyn's attention.

"What did you find, boy?" She knelt down to study the busted, gravel-covered concrete. Scattered over the dirt was a grouping of rust-colored circles. "That could be blood. Good boy, Ren!" Caitlyn slipped him a treat before scratching his neck and patting his lean shoulder. When Mara exited the salon, Caitlyn called her over.

"Find somethin'?"

Caitlyn pointed at the ground next to her dog. "Does that look like blood to you?"

"Sure does, but who knows if it has anything to do with our guy. God only knows what goes on in this parking lot." Mara pulled out her phone and called the local PD. After informing them they needed to gather possible evidence, she walked in a circle spiraling outward. "Just checking for more blood spots while we wait for the cops. They'll secure some samples and take them to the lab, but it probably won't do us much good."

Caitlyn nodded in agreement. Even if it was blood, without a victim, there was no telling who it belonged to. "We should drive through the streets of the neighborhood. You never know what we might find. Maybe someone saw something and doesn't realize it."

"Sure," Mara agreed.

Sands joined them, and Mara tasked him with waiting for the officers while she, Caitlyn, and Renegade canvassed the locals. Few people were outside. It wasn't the kind of neighborhood where folks sat on the front porch and visited with each other.

Caitlyn pointed to a man walking up the sidewalk after parking his car at the curb. "Let's ask that guy if he saw anything unusual yesterday."

Mara pulled over, and Caitlyn called out her window. "Excuse me, sir. I'm Deputy US Marshal Reed." She unclipped her badge from her belt and showed it to him. "Do you mind if I ask you a few questions?"

The grizzled man seemed to shrink inside his clothes when he shrugged. "I guess."

"Do you live here?"

JODI BURNETT

"Yeah." His eyes were shaded with wariness and he shifted them first up, and then down the street.

"Were you home yesterday, around this time?"

The man crossed his arms over his chest. "Why?"

"We're just wondering if you saw anything unusual. Maybe a strange car, or a man you'd never seen before. Anything like that?"

He scratched a sore on his cheek. "Maybe. Yeah, it was about this time yesterday, I guess. A weird Jeep-looking truck sped down the street. I only noticed 'cuz no one around here drives a car like that."

Caitlyn glanced at Mara before she asked. "What color was the truck?"

"I dunno. Dark. I wasn't really paying attention, you know?"

"I get it. Do you remember which way it was headed?" The man pointed down his road in the direction it had gone, and after thanking him, the women cruised on. "His description could be of the Jeep Gladiator on the video."

Mara side-eyed Caitlyn. "But the guy in the Gladiator isn't who we're hunting."

"I know. But if we find him, he might be able to give us a clue where to search."

"That old guy said no one around here owns a truck like that. So even if it was him, he's probably long gone by now."

Caitlyn agreed, but they had nothing else to go on. They drove to the end of 3rd Street before turning and rolling up 4th. They continued the up-and-down pattern but found nothing unusual or remotely related to the case.

Mara tapped her fingers on the steering wheel. "Ready to head back?"

"Yeah, but let's check the cross streets on the way back. Just in case."

"If you say so," Mara smirked. They snaked their way through the neighborhood, back toward the main drag.

"Hold up!" Caitlyn sat forward, and Renegade pressed his cold nose between the seats. She pointed at a small car parked under the shade of an overgrown lilac bush. "Look! Do you see that blue compact? Do you think that could be Mrs. Payne's Honda?"

"I don't know, but let's check it out." Mara pulled up next to the car in question. There was no license plate on the front end, and the back end was pressed up against a shed. "Is the rear plate on?"

Caitlyn jumped out of the Explorer, followed by Renegade. She pushed a handful of branches out of the way. "No plate back here either."

Renegade whined and stared at the rear bumper. He barked at Caitlyn before pawing in the air at the trunk. "Hold on, Mara. There's something in here!"

"Well, we can't open it without a warrant."

"Call the chief. If this is Mrs. Payne's car, we'll have probable cause. Is the front door unlocked?"

Mara gripped the handle and pulled. "Yep."

"Get the VIN and call it in." Caitlyn gave Renegade a treat and walked him away from the Honda so he would calm down. If this wasn't the car they were looking for, she didn't want to be responsible for any damage he might cause to the paint job with his claws.

Minutes later, Mara ended her call. "This is it! Sands is

on his way over with the locals. They'll open the trunk for us."

"Good. Anything inside the main compartment of the car?"

Mara slid a pair of rubber gloves on and searched through the interior. "Just some slip-on sneakers."

When the cops showed up, they pried open the trunk and Caitlyn gasped. Renegade barked furiously. The man on the video who had driven the Jeep Gladiator to the gas station yesterday, lay in a sticky, drying pool of blood. His pale eyes were fixed open, staring at nothing from behind his shattered glasses. He had multiple stab wounds in his lower back and had clearly bled-out inside the trunk. The victim hadn't been dead long enough for the decay to smell, but he'd lost control of his bowels and Caitlyn covered her nose to avoid the stench.

"Well, we found Rose Payne's car, so I think we can be sure that the man in the video was Elgin Payne." Mara rolled off her gloves, leaving the criminal investigation to the detectives who were on their way.

Caitlyn's heart beat a tattoo. "Payne must have stolen this guy's truck. Does he have a wallet? Any ID? We can get a license plate number if we figure out who he is. Any missing persons' reports?"

One of the cops felt the dead man's pockets. "Nothing."

"Look into missing persons, then. We need that information right away!" Caitlyn put on her own pair of gloves and reached inside the car. She lifted a canvas shoe. "Prison shoes, maybe?" She held the slip-on for Renegade to smell, though it probably wouldn't do much good now.

One of the local cops approached Caitlyn. "We think

the dead guy is a man named William Tillman. His wife reported him missing last night, but it hadn't been twenty-four hours yet, so…"

"And Tillman drives a Gladiator?"

"Yes. The wife doesn't know the plate number, but we're getting that information now."

"And you've got a couple of guys going over to her house to tell her about her husband?"

"Yes, ma'am. They're on their way."

Caitlyn's chest constricted at the thought of the unsuspecting widow. Her husband's only mistake was gassing up next to Elgin Payne. Payne probably killed the man purely so he wouldn't be able to identify him.

Sands jogged up. "Good find, you two. A traffic camera at the on-ramp to I-90 heading east caught an image of what we believe to be the stolen Jeep Gladiator."

"Did you call the Idaho State Patrol?" Mara asked.

"Already on it."

"We might want to alert the Montana State Patrol, too. Just in case." Caitlyn opened a bottle of water and held it for Renegade to drink. He lapped at the opening. "What do we do now? Are we going to try to follow him or wait until we hear something?"

Sands hooked his thumbs through his belt loops. "I'd rather chase him down, but he could get off the highway on any exit and we wouldn't know it. So, let's go back to the office and see if we can't figure out where he might be headed. Maybe he has friends or relatives in Idaho."

6

Colt stepped out into the sunshine after having the clinic swab the inside of his cheek to collect his DNA. Allison had finally agreed to do the same with Jace. She planned to tell him they were testing him for Strep Throat in case it ended up that Jace wasn't Colt's son. Colt didn't harbor any such fantasy. He didn't want this situation to be true, but he was certain that it was, and so he did his best to prepare himself emotionally and to defend his rights as a father.

He glanced at his watch. Caitlyn would be on the road until after dinner time, and he decided to wait until he had the actual test results before he called. Colt walked the half-mile up Main to his office, shifting his mind to his work as he went.

Raymond Burroughs's file sat on Colt's desk, waiting for him. The folder was an uncomfortable reminder that he had had the man in his grasp, but Burroughs had escaped. Somewhere in his research, Colt read Burroughs came from North Dakota. He planned to spend the afternoon searching for clues as to where the man might be hiding out. Criminals often returned home—or to what was familiar—when they were on the lam.

Wes was finishing a tuna sandwich when Colt entered the office. The whole office smelled like fish. "Hey, Sheriff. Not much going on around here this morning. I was just about to go on my rounds."

"Sounds good." Colt eased into his desk chair and clicked on his computer. He typed Raymond Burroughs-North Dakota into the search field. A list of names popped up on the screen. There was a merger and acquisitions attorney named Burroughs, and a funeral director. It listed two obituaries for the name. There were even five images of different men named Burroughs, but none of them were the dirtbag Colt was searching for. Of course, that didn't mean that Burroughs wasn't related to any of them.

Colt jotted down the names and numbers of the businesses listed and called the police department in Bismarck. They patched him through to Detective Collins, and Colt explained he was looking for a man who had once lived up there.

"Name sounds familiar, but I can't say why. I'll look into it and call you back," Collins's voice carried the peculiar accent of the northern state.

"I appreciate it." After he hung up the phone, Colt called Doug Hawk, the father of the teenaged boy Colt had recently caught at school with methamphetamine. "Hey, Doug. Colt Branson here."

"Hi, Sheriff. What can I do for you? Zach's not in trouble again, is he?"

"No. But I wanted your brother's phone number if you don't mind. I need to ask your nephew a few more questions."

"There isn't any more meth showing up at the school, is there? I still can't believe Zach and Pete were involved in that."

"No. Nothing new. I just want to follow up on some things with Pete." Doug gave Colt the phone number, and he dialed Pete's dad, up on the Crow Reservation in Montana. "Mr. Hawk, this is Sheriff Branson down in Moose Creek, Wyoming."

"What's the problem, Sheriff? This isn't about Pete again, is it?" The man sounded weary.

"He's not in trouble, but I wanted to ask your son some more questions about his involvement in the drug distribution scheme. He might know more than he realizes about the operation."

"The lab blew up. I figured the whole thing ended then."

"If only it were that simple. The crime syndicates that run these operations take the hit and then open somewhere else. It's like a plague. Pete was on the outer fringe, but I want to know who's running the show. I have a good idea who it is, but I need some solid proof."

Greg Hawk hesitated before he answered. Colt understood. He wouldn't want *his* son's life to be on the line for pissing off some drug lord, either. Colt's stomach balled up. The fleeting—*if I were a parent*—thought no longer seemed hypothetical. Colt would do everything he could to keep Jace as far away from the drug scene as possible.

For the first time in his life, Colt saw kids from a true parent's perspective.

He cleared his throat. "I understand your concern, and I won't put Pete in any danger. I simply need him to point me in the right direction."

"Are you going to make him testify at some trial? Drug dealers have killed people for less."

Colt couldn't argue that fact, and witness protection for a minor included the whole family. He ran his hand over his face, torn between keeping the boy safe and shutting down this particular drug-pushing tentacle. "I might. But if it comes to that, we can protect him."

"I don't know, Sheriff."

"Well, at this point, it's not about testifying. I just need some information from him. Pete might not even be able to help me, but if he can confirm a few things, it sure would help. I know, as a father, you want these drugs off the street too. We need to protect our kids."

Greg grumbled under his breath. "Okay, Sheriff. You can talk to him when he gets home from school, but I'll be right here with him. If I think you're going too far, I'll put an end to it. Deal?"

"Of course. Thank you. But if I feel it's necessary, I'd like to come up and talk with Pete in person." Colt arranged for a time later in the day to call the boy back. He'd call Caitlyn after he interviewed the kid, just in case. As a Deputy US Marshal, she'd know the process of getting the Hawk family into witness protection. If they forced Pete to testify against Garza and his mob connections, the Hawks would need the WITSEC service. Colt's stomach rebelled like he'd eaten something fried in rancid oil. The possibility of being a parent put an entirely different spin on how he viewed law enforcement.

THE US DEPUTY Marshals left the investigation in the capable hands of the Spokane Police Department and returned to their own offices to research and organize a manhunt for Elgin Payne.

Caitlyn opened the back door of Mara's Explorer for Renegade to load up before she slid into the shotgun seat. Mara sat behind the steering wheel and rested her head back against the padded leather. "We've got to catch this guy. As far as we know, Payne hadn't killed before, but now that he's started, it seems like he's developed a taste for it."

Caitlyn agreed. "Unless there is some unknown connection between our convict and the victim, Payne likely murdered the guy just because he saw Payne's face. That's hardcore."

"We wouldn't have found the body so soon if you hadn't insisted on driving through the neighborhood." Mara reached back and scratched under Renegade's chin. He groaned with pleasure and nuzzled her ear. "And if it weren't for your dog, we also wouldn't have known about the dead guy until investigators went through the car at the impound lot. Both those things give us a slight jump in time."

"We need to figure out where Payne is headed." Caitlyn snapped on her seatbelt. "And the sooner, the better."

"How long will you remain attached to our office? We

could sure use Renegade's and your help to see this through."

Caitlyn rolled her tense shoulders. The question Mara asked was the rub. She'd originally thought this would be a simple tracking case that would last maybe two or three days. Now, it looked like a serious manhunt, and who knew how long that commitment would be? Colt was home dealing with the likelihood of being a father, and McKenzie wanted her to help with the wedding festivities. But in good conscience, Caitlyn couldn't leave the hunt when a dangerous murderer was out on the streets. "I'll stay as long as it takes."

Mara grinned and held her fist up for a bump. "Awesome. I must admit it's nice to have another woman in the office, too. The guys are great, but... you know." The women shared a knowing smile, and Mara drove them back to the US Marshals Office. "Looks like we're in for a late night. Do you have a place to stay?"

"No. I came right here. I'll call around, though." Caitlyn googled motels in Spokane that allowed dogs.

Mara glanced at Caitlyn's phone screen. "Why don't you bunk at my place tonight? You're welcome to stay as long as you're in town."

"Thanks, that's a nice offer." Caitlyn rested her phone on her knee. "And I might take you up on it if I end up needing to stay here more than a couple of days."

"The offer stands."

Caitlyn's phone buzzed, and Colt's handsome face lit up the screen. She bit her lip. She didn't want to talk to Colt right now. Not in front of Mara. Not when they had such an important issue to discuss. Plus, she had to tell him she didn't know how long she'd be gone. She pressed the button on the side of her phone, sending his call to voicemail.

Mara smirked. "Who does that gorgeous face belong to?"

Caitlyn tried to keep her grin from spreading, but her lips didn't cooperate. "My fiancé, Colt."

"Wow, and you sent him to voicemail? Are you crazy?"

Chuckling, Caitlyn shoved her phone into her pocket. "It's complicated."

"Isn't it always?"

ELGIN SPED east on I-90 across the narrow panhandle of Idaho into Montana. He'd given himself a solid head start, but it wouldn't be long before the cops began hunting for the Gladiator he escaped in. They wouldn't know to search for the guy he'd left in the trunk of Rose's car for at least 24 hours, unless they found the Honda by some fluke of luck. In which case, the chase would heat up.

His nervous system hummed. The whole running from the law experience exhilarated him. Especially the power he felt when he watched the life ebb out of Rose's eyes as he tightened his belt around her throat. He'd enjoyed the same wave of ecstasy when he'd stabbed the guy at the gas station, and the man's earthy-smelling, warm blood coated Elgin's hand and soaked into the carpet of his wife's trunk. He risked a few precious minutes so he could witness the light fade from the man's eyes too, even as he begged for his life. Elgin only wished he could have lavished in the same pleasure with the bastard who was screwing his wife, but he'd shot him in the head, and his eyes were part of the gore left on the bedroom wall. A slow grin slid across Elgin's mouth at the memory. Who knew murder could be so fulfilling?

Elgin shook himself out of his reverie. He'd been zoning out too often and needed to stay in control, so he turned his focus to driving where he was going as fast as possible without getting pulled over. He needed his meds and there was only one place he could get them without alerting the interstate prescription drug database. Unsure if they tracked his kind of meds on that system or not, Elgin decided it wasn't worth the risk.

About ten miles before the city of Missoula, he exited the highway and searched the small-town neighborhood for another getaway car that would take him home.

7

McKenzie watched out the window of the Reeds' great room for Dylan. He was late for supper, and she was weary of running interference between his parents all day. Dylan's dog trotted into the barnyard, and McKenzie headed toward the kitchen. "I see Larry. I bet Dylan isn't far behind. I'll go tell him dinner is waiting." Before either Stella or John had a chance to respond, she flew through the kitchen and out the back door.

Dylan led his big Quarter Horse, Sampson, around from the back of the barn and in through the sliding door. McKenzie hurried to join them. "You're late," she said as she inhaled the comforting scent of dried hay and leather that permeated the outbuilding.

Dylan held his horse's front hoof in his hand and looked up at her as she rounded the doorway. "Well, hello to you too." He grinned. "I didn't realize I was punching a clock."

"Sorry. Hello." She kissed the soft whiskers on his cheek. "You're not on the clock, but your parents have been arguing and snapping at each other all day, and I've been wishing you were home since noon."

"They've been fighting?" His dark brows scrunched together. "What about? They never fight."

McKenzie rocked back on her heels and crossed her arms. "They're pretty good at it, for not having any practice. Primarily, they disagree on how to spend their retirement years."

"Oh. Yeah. I have heard some grumbling about that. That's when I head outside."

McKenzie gave him a wry look and changed the subject. "Is something wrong with Sampson?"

Dylan released the horse's foot. "No, I think he's alright. He threw a shoe and chipped off a big chunk of his hoof. That's why I'm late. I didn't want to risk hurting him, so I hand-walked him home. I just need to smooth out the edges and put on a new shoe. Then I'll be in."

"Do you have to do it right now? Dinner's waiting."

A shadow passed through Dylan's eyes, and he lowered his gaze to his horse's foot. "The animals on a ranch have to come first," he murmured. "I would have thought you, of all people, would understand that."

Defensiveness choked her answer. "Of course, I do. But you said he wasn't hurt."

"And I'd like to keep it that way."

"Look, I've had enough of people snapping at each other today. I don't need it from you, too." McKenzie was about to spin on her heel and stomp toward her car, but her ringtone chirped from her pocket. She slid it out. The caller was Tony Cross, the head of the Escambia County Police K9 Unit down in Florida, and a long-time friend. The last time she'd talked to him, she'd told him she was staying in Moose Creek for good and starting a dog breeding and training business. He'd been surprised, and less than thrilled, to hear about her relationship with Dylan. Tony had wanted to date McKenzie when she lived there, but it never really happened before she came to Wyoming last summer to work with Caitlyn's dog.

Since then, she and Caitlyn had become best friends, and McKenzie got engaged to marry Dylan. She sucked in a breath and answered. "Hi, Tony. It's been a while. How's it going?"

"It's been too long. I miss you." His deep voice vibrated through her phone. "Have you decided to come home yet?"

"No, I told you I'm staying up here in Wyoming. This is my home now."

"I know, but I was hoping you'd changed your mind."

McKenzie glanced back at Dylan. His dark eyes studied her under hooded lids as she spoke. Turning her back to him, she walked toward her car. "I'm not changing my mind. I've started my business, and Dylan and I are engaged. We're getting married in three weeks."

"McKenzie, that's really fast. Have you thought this through? I mean, how well can you possibly know this guy?"

"Of course, I've thought it through."

"Can I at least see you before you make this leap? I... there are some things I've left unsaid."

McKenzie squeezed her eyes shut. "Tony, I'm sorry if I led you to believe we were more than friends, but—"

"I'm coming up. I have to see you. You owe me at least that, plus I can meet your new dogs… talk to you about future business, too."

She needed his business *and* his referrals, but how would Dylan react to Tony coming around? Her friend had always been a flirt—something she'd fielded easily enough—but now it sounded like he wanted to talk her out of marrying Dylan. There was no way this would turn out well. "Now's not a good time for a visit, Tony. Maybe later, after Athena has her puppies." Silently, she added, *After my wedding.*

"Tell him to come." Dylan's voice was low and ominous and came from only inches behind her. McKenzie jumped and spun around. How had he snuck up so close without her hearing him? "Go on, why don't you invite him to our wedding?" Dylan's dark eyes appeared black under the brim of his hat, in the dusk of the evening.

McKenzie's heart thudded thickly, and her ears flushed with heat. Tony's voice startled her. "When is she due?"

"Uh… a week or so," she answered, though, in truth, Athena was due any day. "Why don't you come up in late August or September? With any luck, she'll have a few extra puppies than expected, and by then, they'll be old enough for you to see their true potential."

Dylan reached up, covering her hand that gripped the phone with his calloused palm. One side of his mouth twitched like he was going to smile, but it never materialized. He pulled her hand away and took the phone from her, then held it to his own ear. "Tony, this is Dylan Reed, McKenzie's fiancé. I'd like to personally invite you up for our wedding."

"Good. I'll be there."

"Fine. McKenzie can give you the details." Dylan's eyes sparked with challenge as he handed the phone back to her. "I'm going to tend my horse. I'll see you inside unless you're going back to your apartment."

McKenzie tilted her head in dismayed outrage. She returned to her phone call. "Tony, I'll call you back in a little bit." She hung up without waiting for him to respond. "What are you doing? I don't want Tony at our wedding. If I did, he'd already be on the guest list."

"Why not? I thought you two were good *friends*," Dylan challenged her.

"You know damn well that he would have liked for us to be more than friends."

"Yes, and he wants to come up and try to win you back. I say, let him try. He can come up and learn it's time to leave you the hell alone."

McKenzie gaped at him. "What is the matter with you? Are you planning some medieval duel or something? I can handle this on my own."

"Didn't sound like it to me."

Resentment and indignation forced their way out of her throat in a growl, and McKenzie stomped to her car. She got in and slammed her door. Dylan yelled something, but she couldn't hear him over the roar of her engine as she sped away. Her tires skidded sideways on the gravel drive, and she pressed the gas harder. She'd had more than enough of the stubborn Reed arrogance for one day. She glanced at her reflection in the rearview mirror and said aloud, "I don't need Tony's approval to marry Dylan, and I sure as hell don't need Dylan acting like some wild animal, beating his chest, and claiming me as his mate!"

8

Caitlyn handed the clerk her work credit card and accepted the plastic key and a map showing her the motel property where she had made a reservation for the night. She and Renegade found their room, and she dropped her bag on the bed. After a quick change into some running gear, Caitlyn took Renegade on a 5K run that she hoped would help him sleep. Their motel wasn't in a great part of town, but she never worried about that when she was out with her big, fierce-looking dog.

It didn't matter anyway, because no one was out on the dark streets of the surrounding neighborhood. The houses appeared buttoned up for the night, so Caitlyn and Renegade made their run down the middle of the road. Her leg muscles reveled in the flex and stretch of the exercise. She'd spent way too much time sitting inside of cars all day. So had Renegade, for that matter. His giant stride caused him to tug at the leash. He, too, seemed to yearn for an all-out sprint.

Dripping with sweat when they returned to the motel, Caitlyn filled a bowl with cool water for Ren and immersed herself in a lukewarm shower. After she toweled off, she slid into a large T-shirt she'd stolen from Colt and dropped onto the bed. It was time to make the call. Hopefully, Colt was in a good mood.

"Hey, sorry I didn't answer your call earlier. I wasn't in a place where I could talk. How did it go today?"

Colt caught her up on his conversation with Allison that morning. "I did the cheek swab test this morning, and Allison said she'd take Jace in for the same thing this afternoon. I haven't talked to her since then. I imagine she'll wait for 100 percent confirmation before she speaks with Jace."

"That's probably a good idea, even though we know how the test will turn out." Caitlyn closed her eyes and rested her head back on a stack of pillows. Renegade sat next to the bed and propped his chin on the edge of the mattress. She absently rubbed her dog's forehead and asked Colt, "How was it—talking about… everything?" She hated the queasy feeling that filled her belly when she thought of Colt and Allison spending the morning together.

"Mostly irritating. I wish we didn't have to deal with all this, but it is what it is."

"The thing is, none of this is Jace's fault, and we all need to think more about what's best for him than for ourselves. Though, if I'm honest, I'm struggling a little. I never imagined us getting married and having an instant ten-year-old." She bit hard on her lip. Her eyes smarted behind their closed lids.

"I'm sorry, Catie." Colt's voice sounded dejected, jarring her instantly into compassion.

"I know. It isn't what we expected, but we'll make it work. We'll figure it out."

He paused, and the silence hummed between them. "I love you; you know."

"I know. I love you, too." She inhaled a deep breath. "Keep that in mind when I tell you my news." Her heart constricted causing her chest to ache. She didn't want to tell Colt she wasn't coming home right away. Not when he needed her.

"Is everything okay?"

"Yeah, but this case involves far more than just a K9 search and apprehend. We found the perp's car with a dead man in the trunk. So far, he's been out of prison for about 48 hours, and he's already killed four people." She swallowed against the soreness in her throat. "I can't leave until we hunt him down. I wouldn't be able to live with myself if I quit and he murdered someone else."

"But Spokane isn't your assigned duty office. Don't they have enough marshals there to take on the search?" Guilt flourished in her gut at the sound of the strain in Colt's voice.

"Probably, but the fugitive is on the run. He left Spokane and headed into Idaho. We don't know yet if he is hiding out there somewhere, or if he stayed on the highway and drove into Montana. He stole his last victim's car, so we have the state patrols in both Idaho and Montana searching for it. This has become a multi-state, multi-team search. I don't know where I'll end up over the next couple of days, but with any luck, we'll catch him soon. We have to."

"I wish you were home."

"I know." The pull to be in two places at once caused a real pain in her chest. No one had ordered her to stay on this case, but her conscience wouldn't let her off the hook. "I'm sorry."

"It's okay because it looks like I'll be driving back up to Montana tomorrow, anyway. I want to sit down with that kid, Pete Hawk, and see if he knows anything more about the drug operation on the rez. Maybe he's seen or heard something he doesn't realize could be helpful."

"Are you searching for Ray Burroughs?"

"Yes, and I want to talk to Tito Garza while I'm up there. I figure he'll deny being on the rez the day of the explosion, but maybe he'll slip up and clue me into something. What I really want to know is how he is connected to Burroughs."

"*If* they are."

"They are. I just need proof."

"Are you working with the Billings Police Department?"

"They know I'll be up there, but they won't be backing me up unless I need an arrest made, or something."

"Be careful. No more black eyes this close to McKenzie and Dylan's wedding," she teased. "My mom will want to put concealer on your face for the photos."

Colt chuckled. "You be careful too. Stay vigilant."

"Always am." Caitlyn's phone vibrated against her cheek, and she pulled it away to read the alert. "Colt, I gotta go. I just got a text about our fugitive's most recent location."

Colt dropped his phone onto his chest as he lay across his couch. The Rockies-Mets baseball game played on his flatscreen, but he'd turned off the sound when Caitlyn called. Part of him wished he could time-travel back a month before his life changed forever. But the other half of his heart yearned to get to know his son. Of course, if he was going to time-travel, he may as well go back ten years and never make the mistake that had caused so much upheaval in his adult life in the first place.

His phone buzzed, and he flipped it over to peer at the caller ID. "Blake, what's up?" That the town's doctor was calling him this late at night, already told him all he needed to know.

"Sorry for the late call, but we got your test results back, and I figured you'd want to hear right away."

Colt hated the fact that Kennedy knew all about his dirty laundry, but it couldn't be helped. The only doctor in a town as small as Moose Creek knew everyone's business. "And?"

"You've got yourself a son." Kennedy's voice held no edge, and Colt was thankful for that.

"I figured that was the case. I just needed to be certain." Colt kept his voice steady, but his emotions flew all over the place. He *had* been fairly certain, but now that he had absolute confirmation, his world tilted sideways.

JODI BURNETT

"Okay. Did you want to call Ms. Lopez? Or would you like me to?"

"It might feel more official to Allison if you call her. Do you mind?"

"Not at all." Kennedy paused. "Does Caitlyn know? I only ask, so I don't say anything I shouldn't."

Blake had been in love with Caitlyn for a while and even though he'd moved on and was living with Kayla Irwin these days, Colt frequently wondered if Blake had ever truly gotten over Caitlyn. The thought was a constant rub. "Of course, Caitlyn knows. What kind of man do you think I am?"

"I wasn't judging. I guess, I'm just concerned. How's she handling everything?"

There it was all wrapped up in Blake's concern for Caitlyn's feelings. "She's fine."

"Okay. I'll call Ms. Lopez. Let me know if there is anything else I can do."

Colt clenched his jaw and thought, *You can stay out of it.* Then he swallowed his poorly aimed bitterness. None of this was Blake's fault. "Thanks," he said.

He disliked Blake knowing his business, but the day when Colt had to face Caitlyn's dad and confess that he had a son, would be even worse. Though he only found out a couple of days ago, he was ashamed that he hadn't provided for the boy. It was irrational, but he figured John would feel the same way and be deeply disappointed in him. It would be a difficult day, and that day was coming fast.

Colt began to feel grateful he had to drive up to Montana for a couple of days. He might be using the trip to put some space between himself and his reality, but he could sure use the time to process the dramatic turn of his life and think about his next steps.

He turned up the volume on the TV and went to the fridge for a cold beer. His phone rang again, and he jogged across the room to answer it. Once again, he muted the game. "Yeah? Sheriff Branson, here."

"Colt? It's Allison."

"Hey," he said, realizing he needed to add her to his contacts.

"I just got off the phone with Doctor Kennedy from the clinic."

"Yeah, he called me too. Now we know, without a doubt."

"Yes, but honestly, it doesn't need to change anything. I'd appreciate some financial help now that I no longer have Ed, but besides that, I think it would be best for Jace to believe that Ed was his father, and just move on."

"That might be what's best for you, Allison, but it isn't what's best for Jace… or me. I want to know my son, and I want him to know me. I have rights, especially now we have medical proof that Jace is my son. I don't want to move too fast, but we need to tell him the truth, and I'd like to get to know him gradually until he feels comfortable enough to stay with me half the time."

"Half the time? You want fifty-fifty custody?" Allison's voice climbed to shrill. "You *and* Caitlyn, I presume? You probably think the two of you can offer him a better home! You don't even know him!"

"Allison, calm down. We can cross those bridges when we get to them. I don't want to take Jace away from you, at all. I only want to build a relationship with him. That's it. I want to go as slow as he needs to. We have to do what's best for our son, and that doesn't include lying to him for the rest of his life."

Allison sighed heavily over the line. "I can't imagine telling him. He'll be deeply hurt again after the pain he went through grieving for Ed."

"We can do it together. And there's no reason not to honor Ed's fatherhood up until his death. He must have been a good man, a good dad. I don't want to take any of that away."

"You'll tell him with me?" The waver in Allison's resolve gave Colt hope, and he pressed on.

"Of course, I will. And Allison, I'd really like you to consider moving back here to Moose Creek. You have your parents, and Jace would have his grandparents to support him. And it would be easier for me to do things with him, like go fishing, or horseback riding, a little bit at a time. Maybe he'd want to play baseball?"

"Colt, parenting is a lot more than just fun activities. Don't romanticize it. How does Caitlyn feel about all this? I have to consider the influence she'll have on Jace, too."

"I'm not romanticizing. I'm just saying those might be good things to do while getting to know each other. I'll be there for all of it, the easy and the struggles. I promise. And Caitlyn loves and supports me. She'd only be a positive influence on Jace."

"And what about when you two have your own kids? Where will Jace fall then?"

"Lots of people have more than one kid. I don't think they have a hard time loving all of them."

Allison was quiet for a long while before she continued. "Okay. I'll think about staying in Moose Creek, but I'm not promising anything. We can tell Jace and then see what he wants to do. His opinion matters too. When can we get together?"

"I'm most likely going up to Montana tomorrow, but we can talk with Jace when I get back."

9

————

MCKenzie slowed down to 35 miles per hour as she drove through the flashing yellow of the one traffic light in Moose Creek. The music on the radio paused for a phone call coming through her speakers. It was Dylan. She was still too irritated to talk to him, so she declined the call. Seconds later, he rang again. She declined that call, as well. The third time he called, she answered, still feeling prickly. "What?"

"Why are you so pissed off? I'm sorry."

"What are you sorry for, exactly?"

"Whatever I did that made you so mad. Will you tell me?" Dylan sounded contrite and a little unsure of himself, which was unusual and kind of nice.

The change in his attitude melted her anger, and as she thought it through, she truly didn't know why she had reacted so strongly. Dylan had gone all alpha-male over Tony's call, but that wasn't really a reason to get mad. She sighed. "Honestly, Dyl, it's been a long day. I had to listen to your parents snapping at each other the whole time I was there. Then you kinda barked at me about coming in for dinner and then gave me a hard time about Tony. I overreacted. But you overreacted, too."

"It's time Tony realizes you're marrying *me*. I just want to make that clear to him."

"I can handle Tony. Thank you very much."

"Okay. I'm sorry, Kenze. And I'm sorry about my folks, too. I went inside a few minutes ago and heard an earful of what you're talking about. They've fought before, but this is more like a constant sniping session. My mom threatened to fly to Ireland with or without my dad, and he told her she should go. That he'd be here when she got back. To which she replied, '*If* I ever come back.'"

"Wow, that sounds worse than it was earlier. Do you think it's serious?"

"I don't know. Since when did my mom ever want to go to Ireland? I'm out of the loop."

"Your dad is retiring, and your mom wants to travel. The problem is, your dad does not."

"They'll figure it out."

"Soon, I hope. I hate seeing them so upset with each other."

"That's why I came back out to the barn to call you."

"I think we're all on our last nerves with the wedding plans and all. Want to come over? I'll feed you here, if you want."

Dylan chuckled, and she could hear his grin in his words. "I *am* starving. Maybe after you feed me, I can stay for dinner?"

McKenzie rolled her eyes and laughed. "You can turn *anything* into an innuendo. How soon can you get here?"

"Dylan!" Stella's distant voice echoed over the line.

"Hold on." Dylan muffled his phone. "Out here, Ma," he called back.

McKenzie heard Dylan and Stella's voices under the muffle of his hand, but she couldn't make out the words. In seconds, Dylan came back on the line. "I think you better turn around and come back here."

"Why? I thought…"

"That will have to wait. You've got puppies on the way."

"Oh! Now? How's Athena doing?" McKenzie pulled a U-turn in the middle of the quiet street and drove back the way she'd come.

Dylan panted his words as he ran to the yard. "She looks fine. She's pawing at the bedding—getting ready to lie down."

"I'm on my way."

"Good. I'll get myself something to eat here, but I'm claiming a raincheck on the other."

"I look forward to redeeming it," McKenzie giggled, and hung up the phone. She pressed the gas pedal, rushing back to help Athena bring her pups into the world.

McKenzie drove straight to the backyard gate and jumped out of her car, excited to see the new puppies. Dylan and his parents were together, sitting around the edge of Athena's whelping box. "How's it going out here?"

Dylan met her at the gate. He hauled her into his arms and kissed her, sending shivers up her spine, and causing her to forget why she was there for a long, delicious moment.

"Come see." He tugged on her hand and pulled her toward her dog. "She's delivered her first pup—a girl— and she's a beauty, just like her mama."

McKenzie peered into the box, elated at the sight of a perfectly formed miniature Belgian Malinois with a golden body and black ears, nose, and paws. She ran her fingers over the puppy's silky coat. "Oh! She's just beauti- ful." McKenzie gripped Dylan's arm tight as she watched Athena lick her tiny new baby clean. Another contraction forced the dog to concentrate on the next birth.

After the fourth puppy arrived, John went inside to bed. Stella remained, but an hour later, after a fit of yawns, she padded in through the kitchen door as well. Before the night was over, an exhausted Athena slept while her ten perfect puppies wriggled, squeaked, and nursed. At this point, the babies looked identical with their black-tipped ears, tail, and paws. McKenzie stood arm in arm with Dylan, gazing at the new family. "They're adorable, don't you think?"

"Sure are. Are they all spoken for?"

She smiled up at him and ran her fingertips over his dark beard. "Don't tell me you want to keep one of *these* puppies, too."

"Of course, I do." He chuckled. "But I'm asking in regard to your new business. Looks like you have a healthy start."

"It sure does. And yes, all these pups are reserved." McKenzie smiled down at her brood. "Before Caitlyn left,

I asked her to consider breeding Renegade to Athena the next time around."

"They'd have incredible puppies."

"That's what I think too, but Caitlyn's hesitant because she doesn't know Renegade's bloodlines. But, if I keep them for at least six months and get them trained with obedience and drug tracking, I'd be able to sell them for ten to fifteen grand a piece."

"Wow." Dylan counted the puppies. "There are ten pups in this litter. That would mean a hundred grand."

"Minus expenses. There are food and vet costs, and the drug-sniffing kits aren't cheap either." McKenzie leaned into Dylan and gave him a coy smile. "I could use a training obstacle course like Caitlyn's, too."

He pulled her close. "Next, you'll be having me build you some kennels back behind the barn."

"I was going to wait until *after* the wedding before I sprang that one on you." She giggled and pressed up on her toes to kiss him.

"I think you've got a great business going here. Especially, if you don't have to pay a stud fee."

"I'm willing to pay Caitlyn a fee, if I can get her to go along with it."

"She won't take it. And once she sees these little guys, she'll be all over it."

From somewhere inside the house, a door slammed. Dylan stared at the back door, listening. "Wonder which one of them is sleeping in the doghouse tonight?"

"I have no doubt it's your mom. I can't see your dad giving up his bed."

"Maybe we should ship them both off on a long vacation just so we can have some peace."

McKenzie smiled up at him, but her belly churned with concern. Stella and John had always seemed so steady. She hated seeing family upheaval so close to the wedding. "I hope they work it out soon."

10

Caitlyn and Renegade were up early the next morning. They went for another run before stopping by the free continental breakfast offered in the motel's lobby. She scooped a spoonful of questionable scrambled eggs into a paper bowl for Ren and filled her plate with the same, along with bacon and seasoned home-style hash browns. She snagged a bottle of orange juice, and they sat outside to eat.

The whole time, Caitlyn mulled over what little information they had about Elgin Payne and where he might be headed. Last night, Chief Styles texted a group update on Payne's last known location. He had raced through a yellow light that turned red, and the intersection camera caught him on film. The image was remarkably clear, and the facial recognition software confirmed the driver was Payne. The license plate caught by the second camera led them to an address in a small town outside of Missoula. If he was smart, Payne would dump the car he was driving soon. But hopefully, the police would find him first. For now, at least they knew he was in Montana.

After swallowing her last bite of the watery eggs, she took Renegade back to their room for his real breakfast, and so she could shower and dress.

The sun glinted off the US Marshals Building in Spokane, and Caitlyn squinted her eyes against the glare. She parked next to Mara's SUV. "Let's get to work, Ren." He jumped down from the seat and sat patiently while she clipped a leash to his vest.

The office was only half full when she entered. Styles pointed her to a desk. "You can use this computer while you're here. Like I said in my text, we know Payne was in Missoula last night. Let's figure out where he's going from there."

Mara came out of the break room carrying two cups of coffee and handed one to Caitlyn. "Ready to go hunting?"

"Thanks." Caitlyn reached for the mug Mara offered and smelled the dark roast. "Let's do it."

"Good morning, Renegade." Mara patted his head. He wagged his tail and gave her a toothy Malinois grin. "Hopefully, we'll have a job for you to do, soon."

"Yeah, I don't know how much help a K9 team is in this situation, but I'm happy to help research Payne's friends and family until we can be useful. What do we know so far?"

"Not much. We know that he and his wife got their marriage license in Utah, but I have found no record of where or when they actually had their ceremony."

"Utah's a big state."

"Tell me about it." Mara sat at the desk facing Caitlyn's. "He must have lived there at one time, though. I'm betting that's where he's headed now. It makes sense."

"I agree. Let's work on that premise and dig into it. He has to show up somewhere. What's his social security number? Did he ever pay taxes in Utah?" Caitlyn settled into the desk chair. This was the tedious part of the job, but without it, they'd have nothing to go on.

Mara handed her a printout of Payne's personal information they got from his prison record, and Caitlyn went to work on her search. Renegade eased himself onto the floor and rolled to his side with a groan.

"Sorry, boy." Caitlyn bent to run her hand from his silky head to his hip. "Unless we find something soon, you're going to have a long, boring day."

EVERYONE AT THE REED RANCH, besides Athena and her constantly hungry puppies, slept in. Dylan had claimed his raincheck before they slept last night, and McKenzie remained tucked in his arm with her cheek resting on the dark curls of his chest as the morning sun peeked in through the shutters. She blinked her heavy eyelids open and checked the clock on Dylan's nightstand. 7:33 a.m.

A douse of cold apprehension zipped through her veins. 7:30 was a late start on the ranch, and McKenzie didn't want to be caught in Dylan's bedroom. It wasn't that John and Stella hadn't figured out that she was sleeping with their son, but Dylan's parents had conservative values. So, even though she and Dylan were engaged, it would still be mortifying to get caught in Dylan's bed under his parents' roof.

If she was quick, McKenzie could slip down to Caitlyn's old room, and everyone could pretend that's where she slept. She slid into Dylan's discarded black chambray shirt and grabbed the few pieces of her own clothing she found scattered across the floor. Holding them in a bundle against her chest, she carefully opened his door a crack, and peeked out into the upstairs hallway. All clear.

As fast as she could, McKenzie darted to the end of the hall where Caitlyn slept as a girl. She ducked in through the door and eased it shut, careful not to make a sound.

"What time is it?" Stella's sleepy voice caused McKenzie to squeal.

She spun around, still gripping her clothes. "Stella! I—"

"Didn't expect me to be here?" Her blue eyes twinkled in the morning light. "Sorry to startle you." Stella's gaze panned down over McKenzie's bare legs and feet.

"Um…"

"I wasn't born yesterday, dear."

"No, I guess not. Why are you here? Are you and John still arguing?"

Stella pushed herself up and leaned back against her pillow and the headboard. She pulled the covers up and spread them smoothly across her lap. "I'm done fighting. John refuses to understand my desire to travel and see the world, so what's the point?"

McKenzie dumped her clothes into a chair and sat on the edge of the bed. "Maybe after he has a couple of months to settle into retirement, he'll want to go on some of your adventures."

"So, you're on his side?" Stella's brows knit together over hurt eyes.

McKenzie rested her hand over Stella's. "It's not about sides. It's about loving you both, and not wanting to see you fighting all the time."

"I can understand that he wants to rest a little while, but when do *I* get to rest? He expects me to keep doing the work I've always done, while he puts his feet up. That doesn't seem fair. Why can't we go on an adventure, and he can rest when we get home?"

McKenzie didn't know how to respond to that. She saw the logic in Stella's argument, too. "I don't have the answer, but I know you two will figure it out. You have to." She squeezed Stella's hand.

The bedroom door swung open and bounced against the wall behind it. Dylan filled the entry wearing nothing but a black pair of Under Armour briefs. "Here you are." His lascivious grin meant for McKenzie straightened into Sunday School innocence in a flash. "Mom, what are you doing in here?" He cleared his throat.

Stella lifted an imperious brow at her oldest son. "Please put some clothes on, Dylan. We have company." She flipped the covers back and shooed McKenzie out of the way, but not before McKenzie saw a slight smile under Stella's sparkling eyes. "I'm going to make breakfast, and I expect to see you both downstairs in five minutes."

"Don't underestimate me, Mama. That's plenty of time," Dylan teased.

But Stella wasn't to be outdone. "If that's so, then McKenzie should find someone else to marry before it's too late." She slapped his bare belly with the back of her hand as she walked past him out the door.

Dylan's mouth had fallen open, and he swung his gaze to McKenzie. "I can't believe she just said that."

"Serves you right. Now go get dressed. I, for one, am not taking any longer than my allotted five minutes!" McKenzie pushed him out the door and closed it behind him. She threw on her clothes and raked her fingers through her long hair. Sweeping it up, she bunched it into a messy bun.

She ran down the curving staircase that spilled out into the great room and dashed through the swinging kitchen door. "What can I do to help?" she asked, but drew up short when she entered the room. Stella was stirring pancake batter with an angry swirling motion and John, who sat at the table, snapped his Angler magazine open in front of his face. "Good morning, John."

Staying hidden behind his periodical, John murmured, "Mornin'."

The morning couldn't possibly get any more awkward, so McKenzie poured herself a cup of coffee and leaned against the counter. "Has anyone checked on the puppies?" When no one answered, she made her escape to the backyard. She perched on the end of the picnic table and watched Athena bathe her mostly sleeping newborns.

Dylan's broad, warm hand slid across her shoulders before he pulled her into him. "Hiding?"

"Absolutely." McKenzie wrinkled her face into a grimace. "You?"

"Yep."

A pan clattered inside the house. "I don't recall asking

for your permission, John Reed. I'm going, with or without you, the day after Dylan and McKenzie's wedding. And honestly, at this point, I'm just fine if it's without you."

John's voice followed Stella's. "What're you doing with the pancake batter?"

"Pouring it out. If you're hungry, you can make your own." A cupboard door slammed, and silence fell.

Dylan rolled his lower lip between his teeth and bit down, reminding McKenzie of Caitlyn. "Uh… Want to drive to town and get breakfast with me at the café?"

11

C olt spent the warm summer morning driving up to the Crow Reservation in Montana. Greg Hawk had agreed to let Colt interview his son, as long as he could be present, too. Which was fine with Colt, since he wasn't after Pete. The boy had already faced the consequences and punishment for dealing meth to his cousin in Moose Creek. His father had taken care of that. Briefly, Colt considered how *he* might handle finding out his son got mixed up in drugs. And those thoughts threw him straight into worrying that he was nowhere near ready to be a dad.

Colt drove onto the reservation, and since he was not planning on arresting anyone, he didn't bother to stop at the Crow Police Department. He parked next to an old beat-up truck in the dirt yard of a small, tattered home, and double-checked the address to be sure he was in the right place. Mr. Hawk stepped out of the front door and held up a hand in greeting. Colt nodded to him, picked up the black notebook he'd brought, and climbed out of his Jeep.

"Mr. Hawk. It's good to see you." He approached the man.

"You too, Sheriff Branson." Pete's dad was a hulking man who stood a head taller than Colt.

"Thanks for letting me speak with your son. I'll be brief." The men shook hands, and Colt followed Mr. Hawk inside to a tidy sitting room furnished with worn, unmatched furniture. Pete sat in an overstuffed chair next to the sofa, staring at the floor.

"Peter, stand for our company, and shake the man's hand." Mr. Hawk's tone was quiet but commanding, and his son did as he was told.

Colt sat on the edge of the couch near the young man. "Pete, you're not in trouble. I just need to ask you a few questions about how you got the meth you shared with your cousin Zach. Okay?"

The boy's dark eyes watched from under a thick row of long black lashes. He bobbed his chin before returning his gaze to the floor.

"I believe your teacher, Mrs. Smith, gave you some meth to sell to your friends. Is that right?" Pete nodded; his jaw flexed. Colt continued, "Did you know her real name was Elaine Woodrow?"

"No. She told us it was Mrs. Smith."

"Will you walk me through how Mrs. Smith got you involved in her drug business?"

Pete swallowed hard and gripped his hands together between his knees. "One day, after the passing bell, she asked me to stay behind. I figured I was in trouble for missing class the day before." Pete's eyes darted to his father and back. "But she said she had something for me. She gave me a little bag of candy... well, I thought it was candy... and she told me to try it."

"And did you?"

The boy nodded. "I wish I never did," he murmured.

"When did she approach you the next time?" Colt felt for the kid. Pete looked like he carried the weight of the whole mess on his thin shoulders.

"About a week later. She asked if I wanted more, and I said I did. She kept giving me more for a couple of months. Eventually, I *needed* more, whether or not I wanted it."

Mr. Hawk rested a large hand on his son's shoulder. "Pete just got out of rehab. We're very proud of him."

"Good for you, Pete. That's an incredibly tough thing to go through. I'm proud of you, too."

"I need to make amends now. If I can." Pete's coal-black eyes met Colt's and held.

"You're going to be a big help in shutting this thing down, and in keeping other kids out of the mess you found yourself in. I'd say that's a great service. So, did you go to Mrs. Smith the next time?"

"Yeah. I asked if she had more of the stuff and she said she did, but now I had to work for it. That's when she sent me to sell in the casino parking lot. I was supposed to offer the packets to people who came there to gamble."

"How did that go?"

"Sometimes, people bought from me, and Mrs. Smith allowed me to charge whatever I could get. I had to pay her, but then I could keep any of the extra cash I earned.

Only, most of the time, I barely made enough to pay for what I was using."

A wave of simmering anger boiled in Colt's gut. The thought of Elaine Woodrow, whom he'd known for years as a wife and mother in Moose Creek, pushing drugs on an innocent kid, made him sick. On some base level, he was secretly relieved someone had killed her inside the jail after the drug raid on the rez a couple of months ago. At least she'd never be able to hurt any more kids.

Colt suspected her jail cell shanking was no coincidence. Elaine had been Ray Burroughs's lover and somehow, they were involved with Tito Garza, cousin to Anthony Trova, the Don of the Trova crime family in New York City. Colt didn't know how all the pieces fit together, but he intended to find out.

"Was Mrs. Smith the only adult you dealt with? Did you ever meet any of the men who worked with her?"

Pete's body seemed to curl into itself. "There was a guy with a beard." His father patted his shoulder in encouragement. "Sometimes he drove me out to the casino. He didn't talk much."

"Anyone else?"

Pete took time to consider his words before he answered. He glanced at his dad, who nodded for him to answer. "There was a white guy. Rich. Drives a dark blue sports car."

Mr. Hawk sat on the end of the coffee table, facing his son. "Tell the sheriff everything."

Pete stared at the worn floorboards. "He showed up sometimes."

Colt's heart pounded. Peter Hawk just might be the missing link he needed. "At the casino?"

"Yeah. He's a total ass—" Pete's eyes shot to his father. "He's mean. Beat me up a couple of times."

Colt took a second to study Mr. Hawk's expression. The anger of a father who couldn't protect his son burned in his eyes. Colt leaned forward, bracing his elbows on his knees. "I'm sorry that happened to you, Pete. Why did he hit you? Did he say?"

Pete shrugged, and a lone tear splashed on the floor. "Usually, I didn't give him enough money. When that guy came, it didn't matter how much money I made. He took it all, and it was never enough. He threatened to kill my family if I didn't do better. That's why I gave Zach the drugs when we drove down to his house at Christmas." Pete's eyes flashed up at Colt in appeal. "I figured if Zach sold it to his friends, I might make enough to keep that rich dude off my case. I couldn't let him hurt my mom and dad."

"You were in a bad situation. I understand. I'm just glad you're getting the help you need, now." Colt wanted to encourage the boy's bravery. "If I show you some photos, do you think you'd recognize either of those men?"

"Yeah, probably." Pete sat up.

Colt opened the notebook he brought and spread it wide to show two pages filled with men's faces. Mixed into the group of twenty-four images were photos of Ray Burroughs and Tito Garza. Pete studied the pictures.

Finally, he pointed to Garza. "This is the guy who broke my nose." He studied the book a minute longer.

"And I'm pretty sure this is the man who was friends with Mrs. Smith. Only he had a beard when I met him, so I might be wrong."

Pete had indicated the photos of both Garza and Burroughs. "This is very helpful, Pete. Thank you. At some point in the future, you might need to testify in court that these men were involved in forcing you to sell drugs. Do you think you could do that?"

Pete held perfectly still for a long time until his father prodded him. "Peter, answer the man."

Pete's head bobbed slightly, then building courage, he nodded. He raised his head and looked Colt in the eye. "Yes, sir. I will testify—if you need me to."

"That's great. Thank you." Colt stood and held his hand out to Mr. Hawk. "If you press charges against the man who assaulted your son, the police will arrest him and get him off the streets. It will give us a chance to interview him about his involvement in drug trafficking, too. I'm hoping he'll lead us to the other man." Colt didn't mention that Burroughs was wanted for murder. Pete was already scared enough.

"I'll call the police right now."

"Good, thank you." Colt shook Mr. Hawk's hand. "That's all I need for now. I appreciate you allowing me to talk with your son." He turned to Pete and gripped the boy's shoulder. "And thank you for your honesty and your bravery. I truly appreciate it. We'll get these guys and put them in prison where they can't hurt anyone else."

Colt left the Reservation behind and drove to the Billings Police Department. He had no idea where to find Burroughs, but Garza owned an estate on the outskirts of the city, and Colt wanted to accompany the local cops when they went there to arrest him. If everything went as he'd hoped, the cops would apprehend Garza, and with any luck, Garza would roll over on Burroughs. *Two birds with one stone, as they say.*

CAITLYN SPENT all morning in the stuffy office searching for a connection to Elgin Payne both in Montana and Utah, but hours later still had nothing. She stood to stretch her legs and stiff back, and Renegade jumped to his feet with hope in his eyes, wagging his tail.

"You want to go for a walk, don't you, Ren?" She scratched his ears and neck. "Me too. Hey, Mara, want me to grab you something for lunch while I'm out?"

"Sure, whatever you're getting is fine. I'll eat anything. There's a couple of fast-food places down the block."

Caitlyn led Renegade outside, but then a thought occurred to her, and she ran back in. "Hey, Mara, didn't Chief Styles say investigators in Almira found Rose Payne's journal?"

"Yeah?"

"Do you think they made a digital copy?"

"Most likely, why?"

"Because, if I kept a journal, I would definitely write about my wedding. Maybe she wrote about relatives, or locations, or something. It's worth checking into."

"Good thinking, it sure is worth a try. I've been getting nowhere in my search. I'll call over there and have them email a copy while you get us some food!"

. . .

CAITLYN RETURNED with two Quarter Pounder Meals. The women sat side-by-side at Mara's desk, with Ren at their feet. They munched burgers and fries while they read journal pages sent to them by the police in the tiny town of Almira, Washington, where Rose and Elgin had lived. Rose hadn't been a consistent journal keeper. She had documented two to five days in a row, and then the entries jumped a month or two before she began writing again. But the words filling the pages told a sad and frightening tale of pain and abuse.

Rose recounted time after time how she had tried to avoid making Elgin angry, but no matter how careful she was, he'd found fault in her efforts and beat her for what he called her offenses. Caitlyn's skin prickled at the graphic details Rose included of her many black eyes and broken bones, along with the lies she had told to cover them up. She recounted her relief when police arrested Elgin for burglary, and she had jotted out prayers that they would send him to prison.

"This poor woman," Caitlyn murmured as she read.

Mara bit into her burger and spoke around her mouthful. "Too bad she never got help."

Scanning further, Caitlyn almost choked on her salty fries when she read about a man named Thomas. "Look, Mara." She pointed at the computer screen. "Who's this Thomas guy? It's the first time she's mentioned anyone other than Elgin, by name. Do we have a type-written version of this journal we could do a name search on?"

"I don't think so. All we have are these photo images of Rose's script."

"Damn. I'll print out what we have so we can highlight important information, but we should request a typed transcript." Caitlyn leaned closer to the screen. "Says here, Rose called this Thomas guy and told him about Elgin's abuse…" Her eyes flew across the lines of handwriting, searching for more. As she read, she sat back and forced her food to stay in her belly. "Whoever Thomas is, he told Rose to be humble and accept the *discipline* Elgin gave her —that it would make her a better wife. He assured her that was how they did things in his family."

Mara wiped her mouth on the back of her hand. "What a pig."

"If we find this guy, I'm gonna want to give him some discipline of my own."

"No kidding." Mara leaned back in her chair and swiveled to face Caitlyn. "Does she ever write Thomas's last name, or mention where he lives? Do you think he and Payne are related?"

"She hasn't given his last name, yet. Thomas said something about how they discipline in *his* family, but I don't know if he means his family on Elgin's side or on Rose's."

Caitlyn got up and moved to her own desk and keyboard. She typed in Thomas Payne, but the only person who came up was the historical figure, whose last name was spelled Paine with an I not a Y, along with a couple of men who served in the armed forces. Neither of whom came from the western states. Still, she jotted down their information just in case. She didn't know for sure who Thomas was related too, but she guessed it was Elgin. Though, the two men might have simply been friends. "This is a frustrating search. It's like Elgin Payne didn't exist before he went to prison. Any luck on job history through his social security number?"

"Nope. I guess thieves don't fill out tax forms."

"Right? Do we know Rose's maiden name? Maybe Thomas is her kin rather than Elgin's." She glanced up at Mara. "If he's just a friend, he'll be even harder to find."

"Jensen. Rose Jensen Payne."

"There's a town in Utah called Jensen, and about a zillion people with that surname." Caitlyn rubbed the back of her aching neck. A few scrolls later, she saw an obituary for a Lilly Jensen, but there was no mention of any relatives named Rose.

Hushed voices and the click-clack of typing filled the Spokane Marshals Office all afternoon, and Caitlyn's impatience with their lead-less computer search grew. By the end of the day, she was agitated that she was not using her K9 specialty, nor her K9 partner, to their full potential, or at all. "Listen, I think I'm going to drive down to Salt Lake. If Payne shows up there, Renegade and I will be more help physically tracking him than we are sitting here searching on a computer."

Mara tilted her head and assessed her with her dark, topaz-colored eyes. "I get that you're discouraged, but what if Payne never shows up in Utah? You'd be making a wasted trip. Why don't you wait until we have a solid lead?"

Caitlyn's skin itched with frustration. She sensed in her gut that Payne was heading to Utah, but Mara was right; she didn't have any evidence. Instinct was respected in law enforcement, but in this case, she wondered if Mara thought she was simply trying to escape the boring and seemingly unfruitful work of computer research. Which would be a fair assessment, since she absolutely was.

"I think we have enough to assume that Payne is on his way to Utah, and I'd like to be there, on hand, if the Salt Lake deputies find anything to track."

Mara's head bobbed slowly. "Okay, I hear you." She turned off her computer. "And if you're going, I'm coming with you."

Caitlyn gathered her few items before she and Renegade followed Mara to the chief's office. She arrived in time to hear Mara say, "I can do the same research down there as I can here, and Reed and I can fill the Salt Lake Office in on what we have so far."

Styles chewed on the end of a blue Bic pen. "What if we discover Payne stayed in Montana? Or went to Wyoming?"

"Then we'll go there next, but I agree with Reed. Having a highly trained K9 napping in an office in Spokane is a poor use of resources. Don't you think, Chief?"

He rose from his chair, walked around his desk, and addressed Caitlyn. "I do agree. Thanks for coming out here, Reed, and I hope you and your K9 partner find the murdering scumbag. If you think Deputy Gold will be an asset to you and the Marshals Office in Utah, I have no problem sending her down. But, in return, I want you two to stand with me at the press conference I have scheduled in a half hour." Styles glanced at his watch. "I want to show off the fact we have a K9 working with us on this case."

"And two female marshals," Mara smirked. "It's like you're vying for a US Marshal nomination from the president, or something."

Styles grinned. "Someone's always watching."

"Chief!" Deputy Sands pushed back from his desk and rushed into Styles's office. "We just got a traffic camera hit on the license plate of Payne's last known vehicle, just outside of Provo."

The phone on Styles's desk rang seconds before several other phones in the office joined the chorus. He snatched up the receiver, and as he listened, his face lost color. "I'm sending two Deputy Marshals and a K9 down to assist. They'll be there first thing in the morning." Styles hung up and said, "You two will have to drive through the night."

12

Colt followed two Billings Police squad cars in his Jeep as they raced up the winding road to Tito Garza's estate in the countryside north of Billings. They pulled to a stop in the circle drive at the foot of a grand marble staircase leading to the front doors. Two of the cops ran to cover the back doors in the event Garza tried to run, while Colt and the other two officers approached the entrance and knocked.

A woman wearing a black dress with a white apron opened the ornate doors. Seeing the uniformed police, her eyes widened. "Yes? May I help you?"

"We're here to see Mr. Tito Garza on official police business," barked the sergeant.

"I, uh—he's not available right now," replied the woman, whom Colt presumed was the housekeeper.

"We have a warrant for his arrest, ma'am. I suggest you do not interfere."

The woman looked terrified, but Colt didn't think it

was the police who frightened her. Movement at the top of the staircase that swept down to the foyer, caught Colt's eye. He instinctively rested the palm of his hand on the butt of his weapon.

Tito Garza, dressed in gray woolen trousers and a light-blue button-down shirt—casual attire that probably cost more than Colt made in a month—made his way down to the main level. "What is this about a warrant? I've done nothing to merit arrest."

The officers pushed past the housekeeper. "Tito Garza, you are under arrest for the assault and battery of a minor." Giving Garza's phone to his employee, they handcuffed him and proceeded to read him his rights.

"I have no idea what you're talking about. This is absurd." Garza's eyes narrowed on Colt. "I know you, don't I? Aren't you the sheriff from Moose Creek?"

"That's me." Colt met Garza's glare with one of his own.

"What do *you* have to do with any of this?"

"We'll get to that." Colt stepped out of the way as the officers escorted Garza out through the front door. The younger officer held Garza's arm as he opened the back door to his squad car. He held his hand over Garza's head as he guided the man into the backseat.

At the Billings Police Department, Garza maintained his cool and his self-claimed innocence as he faced the detective across the table in an interview room. Colt had joined them but remained standing. The detective tapped the desk with his fingertips and asked, "Do you know a young man by the name of Peter Hawk?"

"I don't believe so. Where exactly would I know him from?"

"You came in contact with him on several occasions at the Crow Reservation Casino."

"If you believe that to be true, then why are you asking me?"

"How many times did you come in contact with him?"

"I don't know who you're talking about, detective." Garza smiled condescendingly at his interviewer. "You'll have to be clearer."

Garza's devil-may-care attitude caused Colt's muscles to bunch. He'd like nothing more than to wipe the smug look off the man's face. He reached for a photo laying face-down on the table and flipped it over. "This young man. At least this is what he looked like before you broke his nose."

"Come, come, Sheriff. Why on earth would I hurt this boy? Don't be ridiculous." Garza's dark eyes sparked with arrogance. "And I'd still like to know what *you* have to do with any of this?"

Colt snapped back with a question of his own. "What is your affiliation with Raymond Burroughs?"

For a brief second, before he recovered, Garza's expression was one of shock. "Who?"

"The man who drove this boy to the casino parking lot to sell your drugs. Is Burroughs involved in your *family business*?"

Garza ground his teeth together before he answered. "I wouldn't know. I am no longer involved with the New York branch of my family. As I'm sure you remember, it was my cousin who paid that prick Russo to murder my wife."

"I remember. I also remember Russo testified you abused your wife on a regular basis." Colt stretched his fingers out to release his tension. Garza was a dirtbag, no matter how well he dressed.

"His word against mine."

"Perhaps, but it goes to show your history of a violent and abusive temper. Like the one you used with Peter Hawk. His father has pressed assault charges against you for beating up his son. They're both willing to testify, and when I find Burroughs, I suspect he'll be more than happy to testify against you too—for reduced charges of his own."

Tito sneered. "All you have on me are these trumped-up assault charges. I'll be out of here in no time."

"Unless, of course, our men who are watching your house find Burroughs first. We'll arrest him, not only for drug trafficking charges, but for multiple counts of murder. He has plenty of motives to cooperate with us. I'm certain he'll have no trouble hanging you out to dry in exchange for avoiding the death penalty."

"So, why would I help you find him, then?"

Colt pulled out the empty chair next to the detective and sat. "I'm not asking for your help in finding him. I'm offering you the chance to tell us how your *family*, the New York Trova crime syndicate, is involved with meth trafficking here in Montana and Wyoming."

"The chance? If I told you anything at all about Trova's business, I'd be dead before you shut the cell door behind me."

"Not if you're in protective custody... not if we put you in the witness protection program." Colt braced his forearms against the table. Leaning forward, he said, "But that opportunity only lasts until we find Burroughs. He'll get the same offer, and whoever rolls over first gets the protection."

Garza rubbed his hand over his mouth. He leaned back in his chair, and his shoulders slumped. "Even if I knew something, which I don't, I couldn't tell you. I am bound by blood."

"I get it. I guess it's a good thing for us that Burroughs doesn't share the blood bond."

Garza's polished arrogance dimmed.

PAYNE FLIPPED on the TV in his cramped room. The headline news was all about him, his escape from the prison bus, the murder of Rose and her lover, and the curious fool at the gas station. The news anchor spoke to a field reporter at a news conference. The speaker at the podium was from the US Marshals Service in Spokane. It shouldn't have surprised him that the Marshals were after him, but it did.

The Chief Deputy droned on about how they were close to apprehending him. The man pointed to two women standing at his side. A fiery black chick stood next to a second hot woman with a long dark braid draped over her shoulder. Next to the plaited beauty sat a big dog wearing a US Marshals vest.

"With the excellent skills of our deputies and this K9

team, I have no doubt we'll apprehend the fugitive in no time," the speaker bragged.

Is that so? Payne chuckled as he imagined wrapping that braid around his fist and yanking hard. The newscast was from Spokane. *They're so far behind me, they'll never catch up.*

Payne's smugness disappeared when the Chief Deputy said, "These deputies are dispatching to Salt Lake City tonight." Elgin's mug shots flashed onto the screen. "If you see this man, do not engage him, and call the police immediately. He is armed and dangerous."

Payne kicked off his boot and threw it at the TV. He didn't know how the hell they figured out he was in Utah, but they obviously didn't believe he was much of a threat, if all they were sending was a couple of chicks after him. *Guess I'll have to teach them not to underestimate me.* His leg jerked repeatedly, and lights flashed across his vision. His stomach rolled and threatened to puke. *I've got to lose the car, but first things first, I have to get some meds.*

He dialed an old phone number from his memory. "Hey, Gramps?"

MARA DROPPED Caitlyn and Renegade off at a grassy area in front of the Salt Lake Marshals Office before she parked the truck. Caitlyn was thankful for a few minutes of stretching and movement with her dog before they had to go inside and check in with the local chief.

"Ready?" Mara joined them.

Caitlyn nodded and called to her dog. "Let's go, Ren!"

She felt bad for her K9 partner. He'd been cooped up either in an office or in the truck for days now, and she hadn't had a chance to take him on a decent run. All things considered; he was behaving extremely well. She'd take Ren out tonight, after they checked into their motel.

When the trio entered the Marshals' Office, applause erupted. "Here's to the local TV stars," someone called above the clapping and whistles. Caitlyn knew the other deputies were giving them a good-natured ribbing, but her cheeks flushed in embarrassment. The only reason she and Mara were asked to be on TV was to pave the Spokane Chief's political path.

They introduced themselves and met their new temporary team. A gruff, older deputy spread a map of the state out on an empty desk. "While you two were jockeying for airtime, we located the car from the video. Local cops found it on the outskirts of a little town called Fruitland." He pointed to the location. "Here, off of Highway 40. He could be headed to Colorado."

Caitlyn leaned in and studied the map. "Did they find any evidence inside the vehicle? Anything that suggests where he might be going?"

"No, preliminary testing shows someone wiped the car clean of prints, but it's with forensics now. They may still find something."

The Salt Lake City Chief Deputy leaned out of his office door. "I just got a call from the Fruitland Sheriff. Crime scene investigators located spilled blood in the dirt about twenty feet away from the abandoned car. No telling whose blood it is yet."

Caitlyn rolled her lip between her teeth. "Have there

JODI BURNETT

been any reports of stolen vehicles or missing persons in that area?"

"Not yet, but Payne will need some type of transportation, so we're keeping an ear to the ground."

Mara squeezed in between Caitlyn and the local deputy marshal. "Do you have a team out there on location?"

"Not yet. We just got the news ourselves."

Caitlyn stepped away from the map. "Ren and I will be part of that team. Text me the coordinates of the car's location. Renegade might be able to pick up Paynes's scent or track the blood if there's a trail. Let's go!"

Mara called after her. "I'll stay here at the Salt Lake office and keep you posted with any new intel. Hey, Reed! Catch your keys." She tossed them across the office. With one hand, Caitlyn snatched the key-ring out of the air, and she and Renegade dashed out to the truck.

A little over an hour later, after following the map on her phone, Caitlyn arrived at the location of the abandoned car. Yellow crime scene tape roped off the area. She and Ren hopped out of the truck and made their way to the scene recorder. She pointed to the badge on her hip. "Deputy Marshal Reed. I'm here to see if my dog can lend any tracking assistance."

The officer wrote down Caitlyn's name, and the time she and Renegade arrived at the scene. He nodded, and she ducked under the plastic tape. She approached the car. "Is this the way they found the vehicle, with the driver's door and the trunk open? Or did investigators open them when they got here?"

A woman in a white coverall, gloves, and a mask

looked up from the ground outside the trunk. "And you are?"

Caitlyn thrust out her hand, but seeing the gloves again, she let her arm fall to her side. "US Deputy Marshal Reed." She pointed to the badge clipped to her belt and then stroked Renegade's head. "This is my K9 partner, Renegade. We're here to find a trail if Payne left one."

"Welcome aboard, Deputy Marshal. We found the car exactly like this. We're prepping it now to be sealed and towed in for a more in-depth inspection."

Caitlyn took several photos with her phone. "No blood inside the car?"

"Not that we detected, but you never know what will show up under Luminal."

"I'd like my dog to smell the driver's seat to get a scent to track."

The investigator frowned at Renegade. "We can't let him get hair or dirt inside the vehicle."

"I won't let him climb inside, but if you find a few dog hairs, you'll know where they came from." Caitlyn moved past the woman toward the door. Renegade took several seconds sniffing the seat before Caitlyn asked the investigator to show her where they found the blood. After spending some time allowing Renegade to get a good scent marker, she said, "Renegade, *stopa*. Find 'em, boy."

Renegade sniffed around the blood-soaked dirt, searching for more scent. When he caught a whiff of something, he ran off with his nose to the ground. He stopped only twenty feet later, seemingly having lost the trail. After searching nearby and finding nothing, he returned and sat down in the last place he had smelled anything and whined.

"Good boy, Ren." Caitlyn unclipped a chew toy from her belt and let him play with it as a reward while she scouted the area. "There's a tire track here in the soft dirt! Makes me wonder if whoever's blood that was, was put into another car. Can we get a cast made of the track?"

A Fruitland Sheriff's Deputy grabbed a kit from his car and ran toward her. She pointed out the spot. Until they got a stolen vehicle or missing persons' report, or really lucked out and got a DNA match on the blood, they were stuck in Fruitland, guessing where Payne might be going from there.

Two other Deputy Marshals arrived from Salt Lake, and she reported to them all she knew so far. "I'm guessing the blood belongs to the owner of Paynes's most recent stolen vehicle." She failed to stifle a powerful yawn. "Listen, I'm going to go get a room. I drove all night, and I'm beat. I'll call you in the morning." She gave them her cell number before she and Renegade climbed back into her truck. On her way to the motel, she called Mara to fill her in.

"Damn, girl. We need to find him before he kills anybody else."

Caitlyn rubbed her scratchy, tired eyes. "Yep. I'm pulling into the motel now. Call me if you find out anything new."

"Will do." Caitlyn lifted her phone to end the call when she heard, "Wait!" Mara's voice sounded distracted. "I'm re-reading Paynes's prison intake form."

"Yeah?"

"What's Carbamazepine?"

COLT RUBBED the back of his neck. It had been a long day, and he was tired. He reserved a motel room near the Billings PD, so he'd be close if Garza decided to share any information. Garza wouldn't be able to post bail until morning and Colt hoped that a night in jail might convince the man he'd rather give up Burroughs than spend any more time in prison.

On his way to the Super 8, Colt called Caitlyn. "Hey, have you and Ren caught your bad guy yet?"

"Hi, Colt." Her voice wrapped around him like a warm blanket. "No, not yet. Payne leads a pretty good goose chase. We managed to follow him to Fruitland, Utah, but we lost him again."

"You're in Utah?" A heavy, sinking feeling coursed over him. "Any clue how long you'll be gone?"

"There's no way of knowing. Payne is only about twelve to eighteen hours ahead of us, I think, but every hour we don't find more leads, the timespan increases. I drove all night to get down here, so I'm headed to a motel right now. Poor Ren. He's practically jumping out of his skin, but he'll have to wait till tomorrow for a good run." Caitlyn paused. "What's going on at home?"

Avoiding her question, he said, "I'm up in Montana right now. I talked with Pete Hawk, the kid who sold the meth to Zach. He's able to connect Garza to the drug trafficking on the rez, and he also connected Burroughs to Garza."

"You're kidding! Sounds like you hit a gold mine."

He parked his car in the motel lot underneath a huge 8 sign. "I think we might have. We arrested Garza for assaulting Pete, and now our strategy is to pit Garza against Burroughs and see what comes out."

"Did you find Burroughs, too?

"Not yet, but it's only a matter of time, especially with Garza's help."

"Sounds like you've got 'em, Colt. But it's tough timing, isn't it? I bet you'd rather be home dealing with the Allison and Jace situation. Any news there?"

Colt ran a hand over his face. He didn't want to tell her the DNA results over the phone, but he didn't know when he'd see her next and it wasn't information he should hold on to. "Yeah. We got the test results back. Jace is mine." Caitlyn said nothing. Colt waited, but she remained silent. "You can't say you're surprised," he ventured.

"No. But I guess I was still hoping for different news."

A burst of anger flared against his sternum but extinguished just as quickly, leaving behind a stout defensiveness for Jace. "Allison has agreed to think about moving back to Moose Creek so I can get to know Jace and be a dad to him."

"She *agreed*? Does that mean you *asked* her to move back?"

Colt had the impression he was in the middle of a floor filled with thumb tacks. No matter where he stepped, it was going to hurt. "I'm only trying to do what's best for Jace." He gripped the steering wheel hard with both hands, and clenching his jaw, he closed his eyes. He wished he had Caitlyn's support, not her resistance. This whole situation was hard enough, as it was.

After a long moment, Caitlyn said, "I know you are, Colt. Listen, I just pulled up to my motel. We drove through the night and I'm exhausted. I should go."

"Yeah, I guess. Talk to you tomorrow." Disappointed, Colt ended the call before Caitlyn said goodbye.

13

McKenzie sat on the red-checked picnic blanket with her legs stretched out in the sun as she gazed at the summer mountain meadow. Vermillion Indian Paintbrush bloomed against a grassy green backdrop framed by wild chamomile, yellow prairie flowers, and periwinkle columbine. Mountain Bluebirds chirped at each other, while two Tiger Swallowtail butterflies flitted and danced among the blooms in the gentle breeze. Dylan's head rested on her lap as he dozed in his after-lunch-coma.

They'd snuck away from the war zone at the Reed home with Dylan's dog, Lariat, and Bear, the Rottie pup. The dogs wrestled with each other in the weeds nearby while McKenzie traced Dylan's dark hairline with the tip of her finger. She tried to imagine what it would be like to grow old with this man. What would he look like with deep lines around his eyes and gray threaded into his dark brown hair? Smiling, she cupped his bearded cheek.

Dylan stirred. "You thinking of kissing me—or what?" he murmured as one side of his mouth curled into a mischievous grin. He blinked his eyes open.

"I'm always thinking of kissing you." McKenzie bent down and brushed her lips across his.

He reached for her and pulled her closer. In an instant, he sat up and drew her across his lap and onto her back. He braced his weight on his elbow as he gave his passion free rein, deepening their kiss. Dylan tugged her blouse from the waistband of her jeans. His rough fingers glided up the skin covering her ribs, setting off a trail of sparks in its wake.

The theme song of "The Good, The Bad, and The Ugly" sounded from Dylan's back pocket. His hand left her side to reach for his phone. "Sorry," he said against her lips as he sent the call to voicemail and tossed his device aside. Shifting his weight to his hip on the blanket next to her, he undid her top button. The whistling tone of the song rang once again from his phone, and he groaned.

McKenzie laughed. "You should probably see who it is. It might be important."

"I know who it is. That's Logan's ringtone. He's always had bad timing." Dylan pushed up and retrieved his phone. "What is it, little brother? It better be good, 'cuz you're interrupting my afternoon delight."

McKenzie sat up and swatted his arm. She crawled to the cooler, pulled out a bottle of ice-cold lemonade, and sipped the sweet refreshing tartness while she breathed in the fresh mountain air.

"Yeah, she's right here. Hold on." Dylan held his phone

toward McKenzie. "Logan wants to speak to you about the Malinois puppies."

She pressed Dylan's phone to her ear. "Hi Logan, what's up?"

"Caitlyn told me your Belgian Malinois is about to have puppies. Are they all spoken for?"

"In fact, Athena just delivered a litter of ten. But yes, they were all pre-sold. Why? Looking for another dog? How *is* Gunner, by the way?"

"Gunner's fantastic, and I'm not looking for another K9, but Clay Jennings, the head of the Denver FBI K9 Unit, might be. I thought maybe he and I could come up and see the pups. Are you planning on breeding her again?"

"Yes, but I thought I'd give her two heat cycles before I do."

"Well, maybe Addison and I can come up a couple of days before your wedding. Clay could drive up with us to see your brood, and then fly home."

"I'd hate to have him make the trip when I don't have any puppies available. But I'm trying to talk Caitlyn into letting me breed my dog with Renegade for her next litter."

Logan's voice rose a notch. "Seriously? He's such a cool dog. You and Caitlyn have finished his training off nicely, too, I should add. I have no doubt that Clay will be interested in *that* litter."

"That's great news. Thanks for recommending me. Having an FBI K9 Unit buying my dogs would be a big feather in my cap and look great in my advertising copy."

"We'll make it happen. How are the wedding plans coming? It's only a few weeks now."

"Yes. Pretty much everything is done." Dylan slipped the elastic band from her hair and ran his hands through it to loosen her braid. With a wolfish smile, he pushed her back onto the blanket. McKenzie covered her mouth to hide the sound of her laughter. "Hey, Logan, Dylan wants to talk to you. Here he is." She shoved the device at him.

Dylan gave her a mock glare as he took the phone. He slid out of his shirt while he talked, and McKenzie listened to the one-sided conversation as she ran her fingertips over the muscles of his back, watching them tense and ripple under her touch.

"Everything's good, except Mom and Dad have been at each other's throats." He listened for a minute. "Nah, Caitlyn's off somewhere chasing some fugitive. I'll never get what you two see in hanging around bad guys." Logan's low voice echoed into Dylan's ear, but McKenzie couldn't make out his words. "Yeah, yeah. You just can't hack it on the ranch. I know." Dylan chuckled. "No. They'll work it out without your help. Besides, I thought you were coming up early to host my bachelor party?"

McKenzie sat up and squeezed his arm. "Ask when they'll be here. Caitlyn needs to know because we want Addison to come to my party, too."

He nodded at her but didn't end up asking. "Don't worry, I'm sure Mom will call her precious baby boy if she needs you to defend her." Dylan laughed again. "Though Dad could still kick your ass, so don't get too full of yourself around him."

As soon as he hung up, Dylan lunged for McKenzie,

and she squealed in surprise. Larry and Bear responded by barking and jumping around them and on each other. Ignoring the dogs, Dylan wrapped his hand in her long hair and drew her close. She pushed against his chest. "What about Addison? You never asked."

"They'll be here next week," he said as he claimed her mouth and lowered her down to the blanket.

14

It was almost noon when Renegade's rough, wet tongue lapped across Caitlyn's face. She groaned and rolled away, wiping her cheek off on her shoulder. He whined. "Okay, okay, already." She pushed herself up and sat on the side of the bed to wait for her blood pressure to catch up with her position. It took a second to remember that she was in a motel in Fruitland, Utah. Standing before the mirror, she combed through the tangled mess of her hair with her fingers before she trudged toward the door. Renegade met her there, holding his leash in his mouth.

"Thanks, Bud." She patted his head and took the lead, clipping it to his thick nylon collar. Somehow, Renegade understood he had to be on a leash in town. She took him out for a quick walk around the sparse motel grounds. At that time of day, the parking lot was mostly empty, so she tossed a ball for him to chase several times before returning to her room for a steamy shower and some semblance of preparing for the day. She'd had a good night's sleep, and now she needed coffee like she needed breath.

Caitlyn had snapped the last twist in her hair tie at the tail of her braid when her phone rang. It was Mara. "Hey, Gold. What's the news?"

"Nothing much. We've been going through everything; bank records, credit card receipts, phone bills, everything we can think of, but we still haven't found any leads."

Caitlyn filled Renegade's food and water bowls while she listened. "What about the drug you mentioned seeing in Payne's prison file yesterday?"

"Carbamazepine. I looked it up. It's a drug used to treat seizures."

"What kind of seizures? Like epilepsy?"

Papers rattled on Mara's end. "Yep. And it's also used to deal with nerve pain, and in some cases, bipolar disorder."

Caitlyn's eyebrows popped up on her forehead. "Is Payne bipolar?"

"His file didn't say that explicitly, but I suppose it's possible."

"Well, we can assume he didn't have any meds with him when he escaped, but he could have had some at his house in Washington. He might not even need them regularly." Caitlyn paced the worn carpet of the small, rented room, and nibbled the corner of her mouth. "But it's still worth looking into. Just in case, will you run a check on local pharmacies in the area? There can't be many out here in the boondocks. I need to hunt down a large, strong cup of joe and get something to eat while you're doing that. I'll call you back in thirty."

"I'm on it."

Caitlyn went to the motel lobby to see if they offered coffee. They didn't, but he gave her directions to the nearest Starbucks. She and Renegade jogged the half mile there, and Mara called just as Caitlyn received her venti dark-roast. "Hey, this better be an emergency. I haven't even had my first sip yet." She sniffed the rich aroma floating on the steam from the paper cup.

"It's not an emergency, but it is a lead. Or it might be," Mara said. "I found three prescriptions for Carba-mazepine filled within a twenty-five-mile radius from where you are in Fruitland. One in Duchesne, one in Neola, and a third in Tabiona."

"Awesome. Were you able to track any of them down?"

"Not yet. All I have so far are the names of the people the drug was prescribed to."

"And?"

Mara's voice lowered. "None of the names are Elgin Payne, but the prescription in Tabiona, which is a long-standing one, is for a man named Thomas Simms."

"Thomas? Are you thinking that could be Rose's Thomas? The man she confided in about her husband's abuse?"

"It could just as easily be a coincidence, but it's worth looking into."

"Text me his address. I'll go talk to him right away."

"Strangely, there is no address attached to this prescription in the database, but the pharmacy might have one on file on their local computer. Do you want me to drive out there? I could be there in an hour or so. I don't think you should investigate this alone."

"Don't bother; there's no need. I'm never alone when I've got Ren."

Caitlyn drove with Renegade to the small farming town of Tabiona. At first glance, it was a charming, quiet little community that she estimated less than two hundred residents called home. She turned down a road at the edge of town and passed by the convenience-drugstore-gas station combo where the pharmacy was located. Next to it, stood a solid brick church with a tall, white spire. Before she stopped at the pharmacy, Caitlyn wanted to drive through the rest of the town and familiarize herself with the area. As she traveled through the residential streets, she realized most of the old homes had experienced the cold shoulder of neglect. Only one or two of the houses were well maintained. Most were not, but all were situated on large lots that suburbanites would envy.

She parked in the dirt parking lot of an old, worn-down rodeo grounds and let Renegade out of the cab for a potty break. Peeling paint flaked and chipped from the rickety wooden grandstand, and rust coated all the panel gates. Grass and weeds grew in the arena's sand, and the place looked like it hadn't hosted any events in years.

The air was pristine out there in the middle of Utah's countryside, since there was no industry or traffic to pollute the sky. The town's remoteness reminded Caitlyn of home. Large farms surrounded the community, but here there was no infrastructure in the town that kept residents—and their money—local. There wasn't even a decent grocery store to speak of, let alone any restaurants or other shops. This little berg would make a perfect hideout for a criminal if he could keep from standing out.

With that thought in mind, Caitlyn whistled to Renegade. He leapt onto the bench seat in the truck and sat panting, waiting for her to climb in with him. She drove back to the drugstore, ready to question the pharmacist about the Carbamazepine prescription he recently filled, and to find out if he'd ever heard of a man named Elgin Payne.

15

Colt entered the same interview room he'd been in yesterday to re-engage with Tito Garza. Maybe he'd get a little farther with Tito after his night in jail. He tossed a yellow legal pad onto the table between them. "So, have you had a chance to think about the situation you find yourself in? Why it's in your best interest to tell us exactly how your family's business is involved with the drug trade here in Montana?" Colt pulled out a chair and sat facing the elegant mobster.

A smudge of black whiskers darkened Garza's handsome face. Tired eyes glared up at Colt. "I already told you that if I give you any information about the Trova family business, I'll be dead before nightfall."

"Okay, then. Give me Burroughs." Colt drew a pen from his shirt pocket and tapped the end of it against the table.

"What are you not understanding, Sheriff? I will not give you anything on anyone in my family."

Colt drew his chin back. "Are you saying that you're actually related to Burroughs? Or just that he's in the organization?"

Garza groaned under his breath and lifted his cuffed hands to rub his eyes. "Ray is a distant cousin. But blood is blood. I'm saying nothing."

"That's your right, Garza." Colt's pulse spiked. Though it surprised him to hear that the two men were related, he kept his expression bland. "But if you don't tell us where he is, then you'll be the one going down. And not only for the assault of a minor and drug dealing, but for aiding and abetting a known murderer. Is Burroughs hiding out somewhere on your estate?"

"No."

"Then where is he? How do you get in touch with him?" Colt leaned forward. "Now would be the time to save your own ass."

Garza propped his chin on his hands and let out a long sigh. "He has family up in—"

"And that is all my client has to say." A polished man in his mid-fifties, wearing a well-made silk suit, entered the room. He tossed a business card onto the table in front of Colt. "Don't say another word, Tito. I'm Bruce Trevino, Mr. Garza's attorney, and he has nothing more to say to you, today."

Colt picked up the card from the table and stuffed it into his breast pocket. "I suggest you get caught up on the facts of this case, Mr. Trevino, so you can explain to your client that it is in his best interest to cooperate with this investigation, lest he becomes the scapegoat for the crimes of his cousin Raymond Burroughs."

"We'll take it under advisement, Sheriff. But for now, the judge has refused to allow for bail, and my client and I need to have a private discussion."

Colt uncuffed Garza from the table and the man stood. He leaned toward Colt's ear; his yesterday's musky cologne was still evident. "I know where Burroughs is, but before I tell you anything, I need assurances I won't spend any time in prison, and that when you put me in witness protection, it will be in a lifestyle commensurate with the one I enjoy now."

Colt returned Tito's whispered comment with an even gaze. He didn't know how the Marshals Service handled those kinds of things, but he doubted they'd set Tito up in an elegant life. That would only serve to make him stand out—the exact opposite of hiding. Leaving Garza's fate in the capable hands of the Billings Police Department, Colt planned to simply wait until he heard from the man's attorney.

It was mid-morning when Colt made the long drive back to Wyoming, and on the way, he called Allison. "I'll be back in town around three, and I'm taking the remainder of the afternoon off. Do you think I could meet Jace today?"

Allison's exacerbated tone bit through the speaker on his phone. "I don't have to jump just because it's convenient for you, Colt. Besides, I'm still not sure this is the best thing. I've been mulling it over, and I honestly think it would be better for everyone if I take Jace back to Missouri. He has friends there. His school is there. I think we should just leave this sleeping dog alone."

Colt swallowed his ire and pulled in a deep breath,

giving himself a second to calm down before he responded. "We've already talked about all of this, and we agreed you would stay here. At least for a little while. Besides, I've done some research, and I have parental rights, too. Of course, I'd rather keep lawyers out of this, but if you refuse to let me meet my son, I'll be forced to call mine."

"Don't threaten me, Colt." She sounded tired, and he let the prolonged moment draw out. "Okay... do you want to come to my parents' house, then?"

"No. It might be best if I meet him on neutral ground. Why don't we go to Gunderson Park?"

"Fine. What time?"

"I should be back in town around two-thirty. How about we meet at three, to be safe?"

Allison remained quiet for a long moment, then said, "I'm going to talk to Jace before we meet you. I'd rather tell him alone."

"You're probably right. It would be better coming from you."

"Thanks. I think that would be best."

For the rest of the drive, Colt played through the words he might say to the boy and wondered how Jace would react to meeting him. How would a ten-year-old boy feel after learning the man whom he always believed was his father—wasn't?

Colt crested the hill above Moose Creek. He'd always loved seeing the small town spread out before him from this vantage point. Turning toward home at the bottom of the slope, he called Wes to fill him in on the Burrough's case and to tell his deputy he was back in town but wouldn't be returning to the office. He parked on the curb outside his house and went in to shower and change out of his uniform.

Breakfast was a long while ago, and he considered making a sandwich, but his stomach was knotted too tight to eat. Instead, he went to the garage in search of the baseball mitt he hadn't used in a decade. Maybe he could connect with Jace by playing catch, then wondered if anyone had ever taught the kid how to throw? Colt realized he knew nothing about the man who raised Jace through his first years.

Thirty minutes later, Colt leaned back against the edge of a picnic table under the pavilion at the town's community park. He tossed a baseball into the well-worn mitt, dust puffing with each catch. The glove needed to be oiled, and the thought spread a vague sense of regret over him. There was a time he cherished the dark leather Rawlings glove that had been a gift from John Reed the year both Colt and Logan made the high school varsity baseball team. Colt's father had died when he was Jace's age, and John often graciously filled in when he could. Colt knew from experience how it felt to be a boy growing up without a dad, and he often wondered how he would have turned out if he hadn't had John Reed's steadying hand.

Allison pulled up to the curb thirty minutes late, but neither she nor her son got out of the car. Colt's lungs refused to draw a full breath, and the muscles in his shoulders and neck bunched tight. Finally, Allison opened the Caravan door and stepped out. She nodded to Colt as she rounded the vehicle and unlatched the sliding side door. Reaching inside, she took her son's hand and held it as he got out. Jace stared at the ground.

Colt set the ball and glove on the table and stood. He wiped damp palms on his jeans and swallowed, waiting for the introduction that would change his life forever.

When mother and son stopped before him, Jace dared a peek at Colt through a fringe of sandy blond bangs. The boy's eyes, the same hazel as Colt's, were red and puffy. He'd been crying before, but now he stood bravely next to his mom.

"Jace," tenderness filled Allison's voice. "This is Colt Branson." She touched her son's chin to lift his face. "Colt, this is my... well, our... this is Jace."

Colt held out his hand. "I'm really glad to meet you, Jace."

Unsure, the boy glanced up at Allison. She nudged him gently and said, "Shake Colt's hand, Jace."

It took a few seconds before he garnered the courage, but finally, Jace placed his hand in Colt's. Their eyes met and Colt was bowled over with a rush of emotion he couldn't name. He blinked back tears that threatened to spill.

"My mom says you're my real dad." Jace tilted his head and, closing one eye, peered up at Colt with the other. "How come I never met you before?"

Colt glanced at Allison, wishing he had asked her what she was going to say to Jace. He cleared his throat. "I didn't know about you until a couple of days ago. But as soon as I did, I wanted to meet you right away."

"I didn't know about you either." Jace set his young jaw and glared at him.

"I know." Colt had no idea how to navigate this conversation. So, he defaulted to sports. "But I'm looking forward to getting to know you, now. Do you play baseball?"

Jace shrugged. "I'm not on a team or anything."

Colt tossed a look at Allison, who crossed her arms defensively and offered no help. He gestured toward his mitt. "Do you want to play catch?"

Jace's eyes darted to the ball and glove resting on the table. "I don't have a glove."

"That's okay. You can use mine." Colt handed him the mitt. "It'll be a little big, but it'll work for now. We can get you your own for next time... if you want." He tossed the ball up and caught it. "How about we go out on the field?" Colt led the way to the grass on the Little League field next to the playground. Childhood memories rushed back to him. "I learned to play baseball on this field when I was about your age."

"My mom told me you were a good player."

"That was a long time ago."

"Is that when you loved my mom?"

Colt coughed to cover his shock. *What exactly did Allison tell him?* "Uh, your mom and I went to high school together." Thankfully, Jace seemed satisfied with that. Colt made a mental note to ask Allison about the story she told her son—their son—about them. He'd never loved Allison. Their union resulted from teenage drunken lust, nothing more. But how else would you explain the situation to a ten-year-old kid? "I bet all this is kinda confusing, isn't it?"

Jace shrugged. "I guess. I used to wonder why I didn't look like my dad." The boy's forehead wrinkled. He looked worried and stammered, "I mean... my other dad. He came from Mexico."

"I heard he was a really great dad." Tears seemed to threaten Jace's confidence, and he stared down at the big glove in his hands. Colt pressed on. "How 'bout I show you how to hold that glove?"

Colt demonstrated how to catch with the mitt and return the throw before he backed up about fifteen feet. He would always remember the first ball he tossed under-hand to his son. *His son.* The ball hit the tip of the glove and fell to the ground. "No problem, Jace, you'll get the hang of it. Now, throw it back." Jace picked up the ball and held it for several seconds before he rolled it on the ground toward Colt. Grinning, Colt snagged the ball and jogged over to Jace. "Here, let me show you a few more pointers."

Colt spent an hour with Jace, quietly bonding without a lot of words through an easy toss and catch, as old as time. When it was time to leave, Allison approached the chain-link backstop. "You two about done?"

A sharp sense of panic stabbed Colt in the chest. He didn't want this moment to end. "How about I treat you two to some ice cream?"

Jace smiled and swung pleading eyes to his mother. "Please, mom? Can we?"

A hard glint passed through Allison's eyes, but she

relented. "I guess, but we'll need to hurry. Grandma is expecting us."

Colt didn't mind if she rushed their ice cream time. At least Allison was willing to go. Jace had fun learning to play catch and still wanted to spend time with him. That was all that mattered. Colt gave himself an internal fist bump and called, "I'll meet you at the café!"

They sat at an outside table in front of the Moose Creek Café where anyone who might pass by could see them. When Stephanie came to take their order, Colt asked Jace what his favorite flavor was.

"Vanilla." Jace smiled, his adult teeth still a little too big for his mouth.

Colt's chest swelled. "That's my favorite too." Allison ordered a scoop of strawberry.

After finishing their cones, Allison and Jace said their goodbyes and drove away with a promise to meet up again to play ball on Saturday evening. Colt remained at the table, soaking up the late afternoon sun, procrastinating the inevitable. But if he didn't make the call soon, John and Stella would learn about Jace from someone else, and that was not an option.

Sucking in a deep breath of resolve, Colt called John. "I'm wondering if you and Stella are free tonight? I'd like to talk to you about something."

"I'm free. I have no idea what Stella is up to." John's brusque mention of his wife seemed out of character.

"Everything okay?" Colt ventured.

"Fine. How about I drive into town and meet you for dinner?"

Stunned because John never wanted to eat out, Colt

hesitated. "Is Stella feeling alright? I bet she's tired out from all the wedding planning."

"I suppose. How about 6:30? I'll meet you at the café."

Something was wrong, and Colt wondered if Caitlyn knew what was going on. He'd call her while he waited for John. "Sounds good. See you then."

16

"Good afternoon." Caitlyn said as she approached the antiseptic-smelling pharmacy counter. An older Hispanic man with salt and pepper hair wearing black-framed glasses and a white lab coat smiled broadly at her until his gaze took in the badge and gun she wore on her belt.

"How can I help you, officer?"

"I'm not an officer, I'm Deputy US Marshal Reed."

"Just passing through?" The pharmacist tidied the cold medicine display on the counter.

"No. I'm here to get an address for a man you provide a regular prescription for."

"I'm sorry, but I can't give you that information, as I'm sure you know, Ms. Reed." He buttoned his too-tight coat, stretching the ungiving fabric over his belly. Rolling his shoulders against the restraint, he unbuttoned it again.

"That's *Deputy Marshal* Reed. And I understand your resistance, sir, but I already know what and who the prescription is for. I just need you to point me in the direction of his home. I'm not looking for him specifically, but for someone who might be related to him. Have you ever heard of a man named, Elgin Payne?"

The pharmacist adjusted his glasses while he thought. "It seems I've heard the name Elgin before. It's unusual is why I remember. I can see if he's in the computer."

"Thanks. I want to ask these men a few questions, that's all. I appreciate your help." Caitlyn smiled as sweetly as she could. Mara hadn't been able to find an address for Thomas Simms, and Caitlyn knew she could get the information she needed if she waited for a warrant, but she didn't want to wait. She wanted to save lives.

The man scooted a cardboard tent ad from one side of the counter to the other before he started the search for Paynes's name in his database. Staring at the screen, he shook his head. "I don't see him in here. What's the other man's name? I can look for that too while I'm in here."

"Thomas Simms."

Dark eyes rounded under raised eyebrows, and he looked up at Caitlyn. "Tom? Oh, sure. He comes into town every couple of months."

"Where does he live?"

"North of here, somewhere out in the national forest. He and a band of others. They camp up there in the summer, doing whatever it is they do. They're harmless."

"How many others? Is it a group of some sort?"

"Yeah, kind of cultish, if you ask me. But like I said, they mind their own business, and so do we. They never bother the people in town."

"Well, that's good." The skin on Caitlyn's neck tightened. She wondered if a cult could ever be a good thing. "Can you give me directions to their camp? I just want to ask Mr. Simms a few questions."

On a mission, the pharmacist tugged the lapels of his coat, came around the counter, and marched down aisle three. He stopped at a rack of road maps and snapped one open. "Here we are." He pointed to the small dot representing Tabiona. "Follow Highway 35 north out of town, about ten miles. Watch for a dirt road on the right side. Careful, it's easy to miss." He tilted his head and peered out the front windows of the shop. "Is that your truck? The one with the dog?"

"Yeah, that's me."

"Oh good. The road is barely passable otherwise. Anyway, keep driving into the national forest, about twenty miles. Eventually, you'll run into the members. Of course, you might get farther with them if you aren't wearing your badge and gun. They're kind of hippie types, if you get my meaning."

She did but had no intention of leaving her gun or badge behind. "Thanks for the information."

On her first pass, Caitlyn drove by the dirt road. She turned around and tried again. The road disappeared into a hedge of wild shrubs only ten feet from the pavement. She pressed the hood of the truck into the branches and popped out on the other side easily. Twenty-three miles later, a wraith-like woman crossed the track in front of her. A strong wind kicked up, and the woman's worn dress and apron wrapped around her legs.

Caitlyn rolled down her window. "Excuse me," she called. "Do you happen to know a man named Thomas Simms?"

A manic spark lit the strange woman's eyes. "Oh, yes." She stepped up to the truck door and gripped the window ledge. "Are you here to meet with him? Tom's so wise. He can help you with whatever your problem is."

"Awesome." Caitlyn forced excitement and wonder into her words. "Will you give me directions to his house?"

"I'll take you, but you'll have to leave your truck here. There aren't any roads into the camp." The woman backed away so Caitlyn could open her door. "I'm Leah."

Caitlyn searched the horizon and thought, *that explains why we couldn't find an address.* Silently acknowledging the pharmacist's wisdom, Caitlyn slid into a sweatshirt that covered her weapon and badge. No sense in alarming the true believers. She and Ren climbed out of the truck and followed the woman. On their way, Leah pointed out different gardens and community gathering places used by "the folk." People waved, seemingly healthy and happy, if underfed. Caitlyn waved back.

A couple of miles into the forested hills, they came upon a small ranch-style house with a newly built wooden porch. The raw planks had yet to be stained or painted. Leah stopped and pointed. "Go on up to the door. I'm not allowed right now. I'm..." She blushed. "Well, I'm not fit to go near for a couple of days."

Caitlyn's eyebrows inched up her forehead. "Okay. Am *I* fit, do you suppose?"

"You're new, so I don't think it matters yet."

"Okay…" This commune had a definite cultish vibe. Caitlyn stepped up onto the porch with Renegade next to her. She knocked on the door. Footfalls and a scuffling sounded from the opposite side of the entrance, accompanied by harsh whispers she couldn't decipher. Finally, the door opened, and a man Caitlyn guessed to be in his late sixties stood before her. Thick, white hair covered his head and hung over his ears and bright blue eyes in waves.

"Well, hello, my dear. How can I help you?" His gaze took in a full-length assessment of Caitlyn's form, and he smiled beatifically, though she noted a hungry look in his eyes.

"Are you Thomas Simms?"

The man cocked his head and with a quizzical expression, said, "Yes… that's me. And you are?"

She inched the hem of her sweatshirt up over the badge she wore clipped to her belt. "I'm Deputy US Marshal Reed. I'm looking for a man who might live here with you. Elgin Payne?"

Thomas's eyes shuttered, and a muscle twitched in his lower lid on one side. "No. I've never heard of anyone named Elgin Payne. Sorry, I can't be more help." If this man *was* related to Payne, he was old enough to be his grandfather.

The hair on Renegade's shoulders stood up as he pointed his nose inside, toward the living space beyond the door. His body was rigid and locked in a silent alert. "Are you sure? I was told he recently moved here."

A slight dipping movement brought Thomas's white

brows together. Irritation flashed through his eyes in contrast to the smile he kept pasted on his mouth. "I'm certain. I know every soul in this camp. If a new person showed up, I'd be the first to hear about it. Just like I was when you arrived." He opened the door wider. "I'd love to offer you a cup of tea and chat a little while. Of course, your dog would have to be tied up outside. I have allergies."

Caitlyn was torn between her curiosity and caution. She tossed a treat on the floor in front of her dog to reward him quietly for his alert. "Thanks, but I'd rather you gave me a tour of your camp. What's your mission here? It seems so peaceful." Though Renegade's alert gave her probable cause to search, she preferred to come back with a warrant in hand and back up.

Thomas stepped out of the house, closing the door behind him. "It is. These folks are looking for an escape from the fast-paced and brutal world of this century. I applaud their desire to live a simple life, and so since I have the property, I'm happy to share it with them. In return, they provide me with an abundance of fresh vegetables, and lovely company."

Caitlyn followed him down the steps toward one of the community gardens. "Isn't this land part of the national forest?"

He scratched his chin. "No. We're right at the border. I can see where you'd be confused."

No confusion here, Caitlyn thought, but she nodded as though she agreed. "Most of the people I've seen here are women. Do men live here too? Families?"

"We're all like one big family." Thomas smiled down at her, deftly avoiding her question.

Together they walked through the commune, and he pointed out the large white-canvas tents in the living area, the dining hall, and the bathhouse. "Women bathe on Tuesdays and Saturdays, children on Wednesdays, and men on the other days."

"Where are the men? I still have only seen women and children."

"They work in the fields several miles away. It's too far to show you today." He took Caitlyn's hand and squeezed. "I'd love to offer you that cup of tea now and answer any questions you might have about our humble community." Turning, he tucked her hand in the crook of his elbow and walked back toward his house.

She resisted the urge to yank her hand free and continued to play the role of innocent curiosity. From this angle, Caitlyn took in the back side of the home. It was much larger than she'd first thought from the front. It appeared that several rooms had been added on over the years. "Who else lives in the house with you?"

"No one. It's just me. Of course, I open my home for gatherings. Especially in the colder months."

A shadow crossed a window at the back of the house. Someone was inside. Caitlyn's gut told her it had to be Payne. Knowing his violent tendencies, she decided to leave the camp for now, get the warrant they'd need to do a full search of the compound, and return with enough backup to get the job done while keeping the residents safe.

"How kind of you." Gently, so as not to cause any

alarm, she pulled her hand free from his. "Unfortunately, I need to get back to work, otherwise I'd love to join you for a cup of tea. Maybe on my next day off, when I have more time?"

Thomas studied her, his calculation evident in his gaze. "That sounds lovely. I look forward to being your host. I'm sure you would benefit from a day of leaving the world behind. When shall I expect you?"

"I have Saturday off. Will that work for you?" She filled her voice with an eagerness she didn't feel.

Thomas touched her chin and brushed her cheek with his thumb. Caitlyn's skin jittered with disgust, and a low growl rumbled from deep inside Renegade's throat. "I look forward to it. Perhaps you'll leave your dog behind, though." A smooth smile curved his lips. "Allergies, you know."

"I will. Thanks." She forced herself to walk away with slow, measured steps, though she shuddered at the memory of his touch. Every instinct she had screamed that something was extremely wrong in this place. At the edge of the camp, she gritted her teeth and pasted on a smile as she turned to wave. Thomas remained watching her from where she'd left him. He blew her a kiss.

Relieved to get back to her truck, she returned to town. Her fuel gauge bounced on empty, which was odd. She thought she had at least a half a tank when she left the hotel this morning. She pulled into the single gas station in Tabiona to fill up. Leaving Renegade inside the cab, she slid her credit card in the payment slot and selected the button for diesel.

Her phone vibrated in her back pocket, and she pulled

it out to see who was calling. Colt's image smiled at her from the screen. "Hey. I'm glad you called."

"I tried you earlier, but you didn't pick up."

"Sorry. I didn't have coverage."

"I met with Jace today, and I wanted to tell you all about it."

Caitlyn's stomach tightened, bracing for what, she didn't know. "Oh yeah? How'd that go?"

"Better than I expected. It was awkward at first, but I brought a ball and glove so we could play catch. After that, things got easier. Jace loosened up, and we had a really nice time. Though, it was pretty obvious no one has ever taught the kid how to play baseball," Colt said with a warm chuckle.

A prickly green sensation crawled up Caitlyn's throat, and she quickly chastised herself for the unwarranted emotion. What on earth did she have to be jealous about? "Sounds nice." Her voice was tight, and Colt picked up on it.

"What's wrong?"

"Nothing."

"Catie, talk to me. We need to be open about this."

"I *said* nothing's wrong. I'm just tired—and under a lot of stress. I think I may have located where Payne is, but I have to wait until I have backup to do a full search. I just left a creepy cult-like compound outside a little town called Tabiona. I think the leader of the group might be Payne's grandfather, and I'm certain Payne is hiding out there, somewhere."

"Good job. I just asked because you sounded like you weren't pleased that I'd met with Jace. I don't expect you to be happy for me, but I would like a little more support."

"I do support you, Colt, but I have other things on my mind right now." Caitlyn swallowed and squeezed her eyes shut. Her reply was harsh, which she knew echoed her true feelings. She didn't want to deal with Colt's new relationship with Jace from a distance. Right now, she needed to focus on her case. *Okay*, so that was probably just an excuse to avoid the situation altogether.

"Obviously," Colt sounded hurt.

"Look. I'm sorry. That came out wrong."

"I don't think it did," Colt snapped. Anguish bubbled in his stomach. "You're not happy about Jace, and I get that. But this is the situation we're in. I can't change it. Are we going to be able to deal with this together, or not?"

He waited for a response that never came. A muffled sound filled his ear and then a crack. "Catie?" Colt thought he heard barking in the distance. "Caitlyn? Are you there?" The call ended.

Remorse flowed through him. He shouldn't have shouted at Caitlyn. She deserved some time to get used to the idea of having a kid enter their lives. He redialed her number. The call went directly to voicemail, so he hung up. Colt understood her feelings but hanging up on him and then ignoring his call was too much. It wasn't like Caitlyn to be so childish. He'd never known her to shrink away from a difficult situation. *Maybe she really isn't willing to deal with me—us—having a son.*

Colt called Caitlyn again, this time leaving a message. "Catie, I'm sorry. Please, call me back. We need to talk this out. I'm meeting your dad for dinner tonight, and I'm going to tell him about Jace. I wanted to know how you think he'll handle the news. Call me." He set his phone screen side down on the table and buried his face in his hands.

17

I *can't believe that bitch is here!* Elgin seethed as he peered out the front window of the house and watched Leah lead one of the female marshals he'd seen on the news, straight toward his grandfather's front door. He stepped back into the shadows to avoid being seen. *Now what am I going to do?* Elgin rushed into the room he was staying in and found the gun he had stashed in his nightstand. He couldn't stomach that they'd sent a woman after him. And adding injury to insult, they only sent *one* woman—by herself. Didn't they know how dangerous he was? They showed him no respect. Elgin slid the pistol into the back waistband of his pants and ran to find his grandfather.

"They found me. They're here."

His grandfather looked up from the thick book he was reading. "Who? What are you talking about?"

"The Marshals. I told you I saw those women on the news. Now, they've sent one of them here to bring me in." Elgin gestured angrily toward the window.

Thomas swung his gaze in the direction Elgin pointed. Both men watched as Leah chatted with an attractive, dark-haired woman in the yard. And, as his grandfather had taught Leah, she led the stranger and her dog straight towards the house. "Are you sure she's a US Marshal? I don't see a badge."

"Yes. I told you; she was on the news in Spokane."

"Clearly the authorities don't think you're much of a threat if they're sending a woman after you, all by herself," Thomas mocked. "You told me how you dealt with Rose, but now I'm beginning to wonder if you exaggerated. I thought I taught you how to discipline the weaker sex. They need to be kept in their place, and this one is no different."

Elgin's muscles twitched. He needed another pill. "I didn't exaggerate. I made Rose pay with her life for her betrayal."

"Perhaps she paid, but the fact that she felt like she could betray you in the first place shows me how little control you had over her," Thomas sneered. "Your mother did a similar thing to your father, and because he didn't teach her well enough in the beginning, he lost control and is now spending the rest of his life in prison. I'm surprised you didn't learn from his mistake."

Elgin's limbs stiffened and his breathing became erratic. He had found his mother strangled to death in the bathhouse when he was only thirteen. She had tried to leave the compound and his father had been right to punish her, but conflicting emotions flared up when he found her naked and bruised, her eyes bulging and life-less. He hated his father for killing her, but he also knew that his father had to do it. Just like Elgin had to deal with Rose.

A ghost of a smile lit Thomas's obvious recognition of Elgin's agitatin and increasing symptoms. Their mutual condition was what connected them. "Go hide yourself. And calm down. You look like you're about to seize. I'll see what the woman wants."

Elgin dashed to the back of the house. His lips smacked together, and a dark stain spread across the front of his pants as he lost control of his bladder. He hid himself inside a closet behind a rack of winter hunting clothes and waited for the seizure. Thankfully, it was a short one and began to recede.

He heard a knock at the door, and then her sultry voice seeped from across the room into his bones. Sensuous anger flared in his head. If he could get control of himself, this situation might turn out to be enjoyable, considering the message he wanted to send the Marshals. *Thanks for the offering. I owe you one.* He let out a long breath, trying to regulate his system and keep his anticipation at bay.

His grandfather invited the woman inside for tea, and Elgin strained his ears to hear her response. She declined. They said a few words, and Thomas followed her outside. Elgin waited for a few minutes before he crept to a window on the west side of the house. He peeked at the gardens from behind the curtain. His grandfather walked her to the gate and then up to the tent rows and the bath-house beyond.

When they turned back, Elgin saw they were smiling at one another, seemingly enjoying their conversation. A twisted rage snaked its way through Elgin's body. The woman had come after him, *not* his grandfather. She was *his*. Elgin moved to the center of the window, drawn by a sense of possessiveness. Suddenly, her dark eyes glanced up at the house. He jumped away from the window, hoping she hadn't seen him. Just in case, he ran to an adjacent room. And more cautiously spied on her from there.

His grandfather walked toward the house with the woman's hand tucked in his arm, strutting like an old southern gentleman. Elgin's breath came hot and fast. It had always been so easy for Thomas to charm women into trusting him. But how dare he try to take this one?

A red haze settled over Elgin's vision. His pulse hammered in his ears. The woman pulled away from Thomas, and she and her dog left the grounds the way they had come. At the edge of the clearing, she turned back and waved. Maybe Thomas was losing his touch, but why was he was letting the woman escape?

His grandfather entered the house, and Elgin ran into the front room. "Why did you let her leave?"

The old man raised his gnarled hands in an attempt to calm him. "Don't worry, Elgin. She came looking for you at first. But I think she likes the idea of this commune. She's coming back in a few days. You need to learn patience. It's so much better when they come here of their own free will. And when she returns, it will be without that dog. That's when we'll snatch her."

"What do you mean—we?" Elgin spat. "She's not here for you. She came looking for me. She's mine." He shoved past his grandfather and yanked open the front door. "I'm going after her."

"You should change your pants before you embarrass yourself," Thomas said with disgust.

Elgin's face flamed. He ran to his room and changed to jeans. Consumed with thoughts of the pretty deputy marshal, he pictured her hiking back to her truck, and he snickered to himself. It was a regular practice for the commune folk to lead strangers away from their vehicles and then syphon the gas out of their tanks. This served two purposes for the community. One, they had free fuel for their equipment, and two, it left the outsiders stranded and easy to manipulate into staying.

He ran from the house, through the woods, to a free-standing lean-to he used as a garage, where he'd parked his stolen car. Pulling back the tarp covering the entrance, he grabbed a few supplies and ran to the vehicle. Taking a hidden back road out of the compound, he raced toward town.

Elgin parked behind a stand of trees about a quarter mile down from the front entrance of the camp and waited. Sure enough... the woman's old truck bumped and growled down the dirt road. She bounced onto the pavement, and as he'd expected, she turned into the only gas station in Tabiona.

Elgin followed her from a distance. When he coasted into the lot, she was standing outside of her truck, filling her tank and talking on the phone. Fortune was his when he saw that her dog was closed inside the cab. He couldn't have hoped for a better scenario.

CAITLYN'S THROAT FELT THICK, and she pressed her hand against her aching chest. She didn't want to fight with Colt over the phone. They needed to talk about Jace and all the changes that were in store, but she wanted to do it in person, not on her cell phone. It was too easy to have misunderstandings if they weren't face to face.

She opened her mouth to tell him so, when something hard smacked the back of her head. A sharp pain radiated through her skull, and her vision blurred. As she spun to see what caused the pain, a firm hand clamped a soft cloth over her nose and mouth. She breathed in a sweet disinfectant-like odor that burned her throat, and hot spikes of adrenaline screamed an alert in her brain. A body pressed firmly against her back. She tried to hold her breath as the strong arms of a man gripped tight around her chest. Her phone clattered to the ground as she rammed her elbow into the man's exposed midsection. He grunted as she scraped the hard edge of her boot heel down her attacker's leg. She stomped on his foot, hoping to get him off balance so she could tuck and roll him over her shoulder. She tossed her head backward, aiming to hit him in the nose with her skull.

Her vision dimmed and then darkened. Vaguely, she registered Renegade barking and snarling furiously. He clawed at the truck windows. Her pulse skyrocketed, but her muscles refused her brain's command to move.

Black cotton clouds covered her thoughts and her mind floated into an abyss.

18

Colt ordered a tart IPA to drink while he waited for John. *Liquid courage.* His first sip was more of a chug. Second only to losing Caitlyn's respect, John's opinion of him mattered deeply. John had been a father to Colt after his own dad had passed away. In that, Colt related to Jace's grief. But Colt was a stranger to Jace, which made their situation hugely different. Colt had known John before his dad died. *Before* his loss. Colt had often spent more time at the Reed Ranch playing with Dylan, Logan, and Caitlyn than he did at his own house. Both his parents had to work hard to make ends meet and weren't home during the long summer days. Colt hoped that maybe one day he would come to mean as much to his own son as John meant to him.

He took a second long pull on the Juicy Haze IPA, wishing Caitlyn were here with him when he told John about Jace. But he couldn't wait. Not now that people in their small town had seen them together. They would knit tall tales and whisper behind their hands about why Colt had been with Allison and her son, eating ice cream at the café. Her son that looked so much like Colt.

John's old pickup parked on the street, and the man unfolded his tall frame from the cab. Colt stood when John climbed the steps and approached his table. They shook hands. "Can I get you a beer?"

"I'd appreciate it." John sat down and leaned back against the black wrought-iron chair. "And a nice, thick bacon cheeseburger."

"Sounds good." Colt went inside to give their server, Stephanie, their order. When he returned to the table, he asked, "You giving Stella a break from cooking?"

John's eyes narrowed. "Why? Did she say something to you?"

Colt frowned. "No. Why would she?"

A sigh carried John's words out of his mouth. "She's been complaining about cooking and housework lately, so I wouldn't be surprised."

"I'm sure she's just tired from all the extra work she's been doing, with the wedding and all."

"Maybe."

Stephanie pushed through the door, carrying two beers on a tray. "Your burgers will be out soon." She set the glasses on the table. "Men's night out, tonight?"

"Looks that way." Colt thanked her and waited for her to leave. "Listen, John. I need to tell you something, and it's a difficult thing to say."

John's dark eyes that reminded him so much of Caitlyn's searched his own. "Best just come out with it."

"Yes, sir." He took another fortifying swallow; his sweaty palms slipped on the glass. "Remember how Catie and I were dating in high school, and then we split up the summer after graduation?" John nodded and waited for Colt to continue. "And how we didn't get back together for a long time?"

"We were beginning to wonder if you ever would."

"Yeah, me too." Colt ran his finger through drops of condensation on his glass. "Well, it was my fault we broke up. I screwed up and, well... I cheated on her." His voice dropped an octave, and he couldn't meet John's gaze.

After what felt like ten minutes, John cleared his throat. "Obviously, Caitlyn decided to forgive you..."

Nodding, Colt continued, "Yes, thankfully. I had to earn back her trust, and the day she agreed to marry me was the best day of my life."

"And?"

Colt released a puff of air. "And the girl I... the woman... Allison Snow... Allison Lopez, now—she moved away that summer, but now she's back, and..." He was screwing up the telling of the painful story. Embarrassed and ashamed, he dragged a hand over his heated face.

"And you still have feelings for her? Is that it?" John's voice hardened, and he sat forward.

"No! No. It isn't like that. I love Catie with everything I am. But... Allison came back to Moose Creek... with a son." Colt raised his chin and stared directly into John's eyes. "He's mine, John. I have a son I knew nothing about until last weekend." He waited for the disappointment he knew was coming. The anger he deserved.

John steepled his hands and pressed the tips of his

fingers against his mouth as he took in the shocking news. "Does Caitlyn know?"

"Yes, of course. Though she had to leave for work before we had much of a chance to talk about it. She's upset, understandably. So am I, but I can't deny the truth. And now, I have a whole new set of responsibilities that neither Catie, nor I, expected. I want to be in the boy's life, John. He needs a father."

"When does Caitlyn get back?"

"She'll be gone until they catch the fugitive they're chasing. I think they're close, though, so hopefully in the next few days."

"The two of you have to come to terms with all of this, and it won't be easy. I'm here if you need a sounding board, but I'd be lying if I told you my heart doesn't break for my little girl."

"I know. Mine too. If I could do anything to save her from all of this, I would. But I can't change reality."

"And you're certain this boy is your son?"

"Yes, sir. We did a DNA test."

"Okay, then."

Stephanie stepped out of the door carrying their plates. She hesitated before placing the food on the table. "Everything okay out here?" Her gaze moved between the men.

Colt looked away, and John said, "We're fine, thanks. I'll let you know if we need anything."

"Can I get you another beer, Colt?" she asked, hovering. He shook his head, but Stephanie refused to take their hints for her to leave. "Are you upset about Allison and the boy you were here with today?"

Colt glared up at her, but John answered. "Thank you, Stephanie. We have everything we need except for a little privacy."

She raised her hands in surrender. "Sorry. I just couldn't help noticing how much..." Colt added a clenched jaw to his glower. "Never mind. Let me know if I can get you anything else."

John waited until Stephanie went back inside. "What did she mean? How much... what?"

"Jace—that's his name. I assume Stephanie was referring to how much he looks like me. Just like I did when I was his age."

"I remember you back then." A hint of a smile floated across John's mouth. "I look forward to meeting him. You know, the older I get, the more I realize lots of stuff happens that we don't expect, but everything usually works out in the end. Trust Caitlyn. She'll come around." John rested a reassuring hand on Colt's forearm.

Colt's phone buzzed, and he flipped it over to look at the screen. "It's Dirk Sterling. I better take this. Excuse me." He answered the call.

"Colt," Dirk's deep voice echoed through the speaker. "I have some bad news. Caitlyn is missing."

"What?"

"Caitlyn has disappeared. Mara Gold, her partner in Provo, hadn't heard from her and when she couldn't get ahold of her, Mara traced the location of Caitlyn's phone. They found it on the ground outside of her truck at a gas station in a little town called Tabiona. Renegade was there, but he was locked inside the cab of Caitlyn's truck. He had gone berserk and tore the inside of the truck to shreds, presumably trying to get out. Caitlyn is nowhere to be found."

Alarm bells screamed inside Colt's head. His heart threatened to explode through his chest wall. He jumped to his feet. "I'll get there as soon as I can!"

19

"Catie's missing! I'm calling Logan. Maybe he can help." Colt stared at John and forced his mind to focus on the steps he needed to take to organize a rescue party. Fear nipped at the edges of his thoughts, and he couldn't afford to let it in.

John's face paled, and he stood, knocking his chair back. "Where is Renegade? Where was Caitlyn last seen?"

Colt held up his hand to pause John's questions. "Will you call Dylan? He'll want to come with me to Utah, and we need all the help we can get. McKenzie should come too, to help with Renegade."

The older man pulled out his phone and tapped on the screen, and Colt turned his attention to his own call. "Logan?" He filled Caitlyn's middle brother in on all the information Dirk had given him, and then gave him both Dirk Sterling's and Mara Gold's contact information.

Logan's voice was low and steady. "I'll bring Gunner and meet you there. If Addison can get away, I'll ask her to stay with Mom and Dad." Logan spoke with a tactical calmness, but Colt had known him all their lives. He heard the tinny echo of alarm hovering in the margin of his words.

"Thanks, Logan. Dylan, McKenzie, and I will take the first flight to Salt Lake City we can get. If there isn't one tonight, we'll drive."

"I'm glad you're taking McKenzie. If Renegade witnessed someone doing anything to Caitlyn, he's likely dangerous at this point. He'll respond better to a person he knows." The clicking of a keyboard sounded over the line. "I'm booked on the 5:32 a.m. flight. I'll be there by seven tomorrow morning."

John clasped Colt's arm. "Dylan and McKenzie are on their way to town now. I'll go home to Stella and wait there to hear from you. Find my little girl, Colt." His deep brown eyes bore into Colt's.

"I will. I won't stop searching until I have her." Colt leapt down the steps, dialing Dirk's number as he ran to his Jeep. "We're on our way. I'll meet you in Salt Lake City in five hours if we can make it on the last flight out, or I'll drive and be there in nine."

"Good. Let me know if you're on that flight, and Mara will meet us all at the airport," said Dirk.

"Has anyone heard anything? Did anyone see anything?"

"No. Still no word from her abductor or sign of her whereabouts." Dirk's voice was firm and unflinching. "But Colt... we *will* find her."

Colt, Dylan, and McKenzie barely made it onto the plane before the door closed on the last red-eye flight from Rapid City to Salt Lake. They arrived before dawn the next morning and sprinted to the gate where Logan's plane would arrive. Colt tensed each time a plane taxied by and paced the length of the window, watching for Logan's. Colt was sick at how he had left things with Caitlyn yesterday. He'd never forgive himself for being so selfish.

Mara met them at the gate. After brief introductions, she caught them up on everything she knew to that point. "There is still no sign of Caitlyn anywhere. Deputy Sterling is on the scene. We hoped Renegade would respond to him since they know each other."

"Where is Renegade, now?" McKenzie asked.

"One of the team broke the window to let him out of the truck. Apparently, he ran to a spot next to the gas pump, where we think Caitlyn would have been standing if she were getting gas, and then followed his nose to the side of the convenience store. He searched around the lot but returned to the spot at the side of the building and barked at the deputies. They say he won't leave that spot, and barks viciously if anyone gets near him. Animal control is on the way."

"No. Tell Animal Control to hold off. Have them leave Renegade alone and wait until I get there. He's scared, but he'll behave as long as no one tries to move him." McKenzie checked the time on her watch. "It sounds like Caitlyn must have been taken away in another vehicle. That would explain why Ren can't track her any farther."

Colt closed his eyes briefly and swallowed back his

JODI BURNETT

anxiety. "What about security surveillance? Does the convenience store have any video cameras?"

"No." Mara's gaze dropped to the floor. "Unfortunately, the town is so small and since everyone knows everybody else, the owner never bothered to install a camera."

Colt's gut tightened into a fist. "Okay, last time I spoke with Catie, she said something about going to a cult compound out there somewhere." Colt perched his hands on his hips. "Have any officers gone out there to look for her?"

"Yes, we got a warrant to search the compound yesterday, and Sterling took a contingent of deputies out there several hours ago. Last I heard, they hadn't found anything. Some residents they interviewed remembered seeing Caitlyn yesterday, but no one has seen her since. Sterling has the leader of the group in custody and is interviewing him now. We recently discovered that the leader is Elgin Payne's maternal grandfather."

"Isn't that the name of the killer you're searching for?" Strain filled Dylan's voice. "Do you think Payne has Caitlyn somewhere on the compound?"

Mara nodded. "We found the grandfather because both he and Payne have epilepsy, and they take the same medication. So, on the off chance, we searched for any recent prescriptions for Carbamazepine and the computer flagged one that had been filled before the scheduled refill date. The pharmacy that refilled the script is in Tabiona. That's why Caitlyn was there in the first place."

"We need to take the dogs to the compound right

180

away. Renegade will find Catie if she's hidden out there somewhere." Colt turned at the sound of jet engines. "Here's Logan's plane, now."

Logan and his FBI K9, Gunner, were the first ones off the plane, and after a quick greeting and catching him up on the details, Mara led the way out to where two US Marshal black Ford Expeditions waited for them. With lights flashing, they raced from the Salt Lake airport, southeast down the highway, toward Tabiona.

Colt jumped from the huge SUV as soon as it came to a stop at the edge of the gas station—Caitlyn's last known whereabouts. Officers blocked the entire lot off with yellow crime-scene tape, and an investigator stepped over the broken glass as he dusted Caitlyn's truck for fingerprints and searched for other possible evidence.

"Where's the dog?" Colt shouted to the nearest officer. "Where's Renegade?"

McKenzie was on his heels and pointed to the side of the building. "He's over there, Colt. Come on!" Together they ran toward the frantic dog. "Good boy, Ren. We'll find your girl. Don't worry."

Renegade sprang to his feet and barked wildly. He jumped up and down, and bounced his paws off Colt's chest before dropping and spinning in a circle. Desperately, he barked again. Colt felt the same way as Renegade. They *had* to find Caitlyn. They just *had* to.

McKenzie called to a group of sheriff's deputies. "Has anyone given this dog some water?"

Milling about, they sheepishly shook their heads. "He wouldn't let any of us near him."

"I'll get him some." Dylan darted inside the building leaving McKenzie to calm Renegade.

Mara and Logan hurried with Gunner toward Colt. Logan asked her, "Did Caitlyn have anything of Payne's she was using to track him with? We can get her scent from her truck, but something of his would really help."

Mara's forehead wrinkled with worry. "Caitlyn used one of the cars Payne stole to get his scent, but we have nothing else."

"Don't worry," Logan assured her. "Renegade will look for Caitlyn, and she's what's most important. I'll get something from her truck for Gunner to mark her scent, too."

Colt ran to Caitlyn's truck, and after checking in with the scene steward, he opened the door. The bench seat was shredded. Springs poked out and pieces of foam and fabric littered the cab. He reached into Caitlyn's duffle bag on the floor. His heart jumped a beat and landed in a heavy, pain-filled lump when he realized he pulled out one of his old sweatshirts. Drawing in a deep, steadying breath, he ran it back to Logan. "Here, this should work."

Logan took the shirt. "McKenzie, see if Renegade will come with you. Let's get these dogs out to the compound."

She clipped a leash to Renegade's vest, but he resisted leaving the spot where he smelled Caitlyn's scent. "Renegade, *Kemne*," she commanded, but he sat down and whined, refusing to move.

Colt knelt next to the dog. "Come on, buddy. We need you." He hugged the dog's head to his chest. "Let's go find our girl. Okay?" He took the leash from McKenzie and tugged gently. Renegade stood but looked back over his shoulder at the spot where he'd been sitting. "We're going to find her, Ren. But we need your help. Come on, boy." Hesitantly, Renegade followed Colt to the Expedition, and after everyone climbed aboard, they raced out to the commune.

The big truck drove through the high grasses and skirted rocks and trees, not stopping until they parked right in front of the compound. Mara parked beside several other law enforcement vehicles that were already on the scene. Officers had all the people gathered into groups and were interviewing them, one at a time. Logan held the sweatshirt for Gunner to sniff and commanded him to search. Renegade sprang from the vehicle and ran, nose to the ground, up to the house. Colt and McKenzie caught up to him and opened the front door. Renegade didn't enter the house but turned and leapt from the porch, bolting toward the garden. Colt and McKenzie ran after Caitlyn's dog everywhere he led them. The Reed brothers stuck together, following Gunner's search around the grounds.

Renegade raced up past the large vegetable garden to a row of sturdy canvas tents and then back down the path. The dog's energy intensified with every minute he searched for Caitlyn.

As they returned to the others, Colt saw Dirk talking with two of the few male residents of the compound. Dirk looked up as he approached, and Colt asked, "Anything?"

"People remember seeing Caitlyn yesterday, but no one reports seeing Elgin Payne. Those that saw her, say Caitlyn left on her own yesterday afternoon after spending a couple of hours with Thomas Simms."

"But no one saw Payne?"

"At least no one is admitting they did." Dirk raised a skeptical brow.

A thin young woman who looked to be in her late teens or early twenties stepped toward them, her arm protectively around a boy. "Excuse me, sir. My son says he saw something that might help."

Colt looked down at the kid's frightened eyes. He handed Renegade off to McKenzie before he squatted down to the boy's height. "Hi. I'm Colt. What's your name?"

The boy glanced up at his mother, and she nodded her encouragement. He stared at Colt before he gathered enough courage to speak. Digging the toe of his worn shoe into the dirt, he whispered, "Bobby."

"Hi Bobby. Your mom says you might be able to help us?"

Bobby peered up from under his blond bangs and sought reassurance from his mother once again. She nudged him forward. "It's okay, son. Tell these nice men what you saw."

The boy shrugged. "Yesterday, when I went to the latrine, I saw a man running out of the back of Papa Tom's house."

"That's really helpful, Bobby." Colt forced his voice to remain calm, though he wanted to shout at Logan and McKenzie to bring the dogs. "What did the man look like?"

"He was tall. Younger than Papa. He had a backpack."

"And he wasn't one of the men who live here?"

"No. I never saw him before." Bobby looked toward

the forest at the back of Simms's house. "He ran into those trees."

"Was anyone with him?" Colt held his breath.

"No. Just him. But he looked scared."

"Do you know what scared him?"

"I dunno, but he kept looking over his shoulder, all scaredy-cat-like."

Dirk, who'd been listening, called to Logan and McKenzie. As soon as they approached, he filled them in on what the boy said. Colt thanked Bobby and ran with McKenzie and Renegade to the back door of the house. In seconds, Renegade caught a scent and took off, following his nose into the trees.

20

Caitlyn came to face down on a musty, bare mattress. Her head ached, sending hot pokers of pain through her eyes when she moved. She tried to bring her hands around to push herself up and became instantly aware that someone tied her wrists together and secured them to a rope at her waist. The realization caused her to jolt fully awake.

Remembering her struggle against a man at the gas station, Caitlyn bolted upright, causing her head to scream. She found herself in a cool, dark room, unsure how she got there. The only light came from the deepening dusk that seeped through a translucent window at the top of one wall. The casing was about 18 inches tall by 24 inches wide. She figured she was in a basement somewhere, and thought she could probably squeeze through the opening, as long as there wasn't a security grate on the outside of the glass.

Rolling her sore shoulders, Caitlyn stood and felt a heavy weight on one of her ankles. Swaying slightly, she shook her foot and pulled. The jangle of a chain confirmed she was shackled to the bed. Hot blood pumped through her racing heart as she tried to assess her situation. She had no idea where she was or how she got there, though she could make a good guess. Her visit to the compound must have pissed somebody off, and she figured that someone was Elgin Payne. Had he followed her to the gas station and attacked her while she was talking on the phone? A surge of relief spurred her pulse. She'd been speaking with Colt! If he heard what happened, he'd be on his way.

But her burst of hope was short-lived. Colt might have heard her attacker, but he didn't know where she was. And speaking of that, where was Renegade? He'd been closed inside her truck. Surely, someone saw him and called the police. She hoped.

Caitlyn's thoughts came to an immediate halt when heavy footsteps sounded from the other side of the door. Keys rattled before the entrance on the far side of the room swung open, bathing the space in yellow light from a hallway.

A tall man stepped inside. "Awake, I see."

"You won't get away with this, Payne."

"So, you know who I am." He grinned.

"It doesn't take a genius." Caitlyn studied the man's form, and by the lump at the front of his hip, she guessed he had stuffed the keys into his front pants pocket. The keys to the ankle cuff were probably on the same ring. "Where are we?"

Payne chuckled. "Nowhere anyone will ever find you, if that's what you're asking."

"I wouldn't be so sure, if I were you."

"Oh, I *am* sure. *Very* sure. And when I'm done with you, it will take five dogs like yours to find all the pieces."

Caitlyn braced herself against the instinctive shudder his words caused, refusing to let him see any fear. "You underestimate my dog *and* my partners. They'll find me in no time, and along with me, they'll find you."

"That's not going to happen. You're alone, and I have you all to myself." He dropped a water bottle onto a small nightstand next to the bed. "The US Marshals will regret sending a woman to chase a man like me. They've shown me no respect. But now, you're all mine. For as long as I want." He approached her and stroked her hair.

Caitlyn fought her repulsion. If she could show the man empathy and make a connection, he'd be less likely to kill her. Maybe she could gain his trust and get him to let his guard down. One way or another, she had to escape this prison. Fast. "I suppose you're right. Obviously, I wasn't up to the challenge of catching you. Were you at the compound when I was there? Was that yesterday?"

Payne squinted at her. "Yes, I was there. You and your dog were too stupid to find me."

"You must have had a good place to hide. We looked all over." Payne's mention of Renegade sent her emotions into a skid, but she kept her voice steady and light. "Where's my dog now?"

Payne's rusty laugh instilled fear in her heart. "You don't need to worry about him anymore. I took care of that."

Before she could control herself, she cried out, "What did you do to him? Where is he?" Tears filled her eyes.

"He's in a better place," Payne laughed. His enjoyment of her pain glistened in his eyes. Caitlyn jerked against the rope binding her wrists. She sprang to her feet and lunged at him, but the ankle cuff yanked her back. She fell onto her kneecap, which made a loud crack when she landed on the cement floor. With her hands tied tight to her waist, she couldn't catch herself, but she rolled her shoulder in time to cushion her landing. Her cheek rested against the cold floor. Payne moved toward her, the toe of his boot stopping inches from her face. He bent down and pulled the elastic band from her braid. Combing her long hair loose with his fingers, he said, "Now, now. Don't do things like that. I don't want to have to punish you... yet."

Caitlyn's skin prickled, and she bit her lips together to keep from screaming. Payne knelt beside her and wiped her tears with his thumb. "There, there. Do you want some water?" As much as she wanted to resist him, Caitlyn needed water to survive, so she nodded. "Use your manners, Deputy."

She swallowed back bile. "Yes, please."

"There you go. Now that wasn't so hard, was it?" He pulled her to her feet and pushed her back onto the small bed before he cracked open the lid of the plastic bottle. He took a long pull first and then held the bottle to her lips. She opened her mouth and drank what he offered.

He spilled much of it on her face and down her neck. His thick fingers followed the droplets across her skin, plunging down the neckline of her shirt. She squirmed away from his touch, and he grabbed her by her throat. He held so tight she couldn't draw a breath. Small bursts of light sprayed across her vision. "It would be so easy for me. Don't you see? I suggest you behave." Payne released his grip, and Caitlyn coughed. "You belong to me now, to do with whatever I want. No one knows where we are. No one can hear you scream."

If only both her legs were free. Or if her hands were loose. Somehow, she had to escape this man before he killed her. Payne stood over her and unbuckled his belt. Caitlyn's body tensed. Was he planning to rape her, choke the life out of her, or both, like he did to his wife?

"Why don't you tell me what you want from me, then?" Hopefully, getting him to talk to her would distract him from whatever evil he had planned.

21

Colt, McKenzie, and Logan sprinted behind the dogs through the thick forest, dodging and ducking under the low-hanging branches. Renegade raced like his life depended on it, and Gunner chased after him. Colt guessed they'd run about two miles by the time they caught up to the dogs, who were darting around a make-shift lean-to covered with green tarps and branches. Renegade and Gunner bounced on their front paws and barked until the humans got there.

"Good dogs!" Colt called as he ran up to the unstable structure. He bent over and braced his hands on his knees to catch his breath.

Logan jogged around him, hardly puffing at all. When this was all over—when they found Caitlyn—he'd have to join her on her morning runs with Renegade to get in better shape. Logan unclipped a flashlight from its spot next to his holster and shined the beam inside. "There's nothing in here, Colt. But there are some tire tracks in the dirt."

Colt joined Logan at the entrance and peered over his shoulder. "Payne must have kept a getaway car hidden in here." He pulled the walkie-talkie from his belt. "Sterling, do you copy?"

"Sterling here," his disembodied voice rattled back.

"We found an abandoned lean-to. A makeshift garage of sorts, we think. Can you send an investigation team up here? We need them to cast some tire tracks."

"On it." The radio went silent. A second later, it crackled. "No sign of Caitlyn?"

Colt bit down and answered, "No."

Logan commanded Gunner to continue the search. His dog made wide sweeps of the area surrounding the tarps. Renegade remained rooted to the spot where Payne's trail ended. Eventually, Gunner returned, having found no scent to track farther.

Colt threw his head back and groaned in agony. After Logan gripped Colt's shoulder in support, he tossed both dogs a treat, but Renegade let his fall to the ground, keeping his golden eyes glued on Colt.

"Let's go to the jail and talk to Thomas Simms." Colt turned back the way they had come. "He knows where Payne is, and he's going to tell us."

An hour later, Colt and Logan sat across from the old man in an interview room at the county jail. Simms leaned back and casually draped his arm over the back of his chair. He gave Colt a sly smile. "How may I help you today, Sheriff?"

MᴄKᴇɴᴢɪᴇ ᴀɴᴅ Dʏʟᴀɴ waited outside the jail with Renegade and Gunner. Logan's dog wanted to sniff around the landscaping and play, but Ren sat rigid, staring at McKenzie.

"I feel so bad for him." McKenzie smoothed her hand over the top of Renegade's head. "He knows something is wrong, and I wish I could explain that we're doing everything we can to find Caitlyn. I feel like he's wondering why I'm not doing anything."

"Hopefully, Logan and Colt will get some kind of information from Simms. We need a place to start looking." Dylan reached for his phone. "I should probably call home. I'm sure my folks are freaking out, but I hate calling with nothing to report. I wish I had good news."

"Just hearing your voice and knowing that all three of you guys are doing everything you can, will make them feel a little better. It's better than not hearing anything. Will you also tell your mom not to worry about any of the wedding stuff for now? I don't want her to even think about it. Not until we bring Caitlyn home."

Dylan's jaw muscles worked as he dialed. He put the phone on speaker mode so McKenzie could hear too. "Hey, Dad. There's still no news."

It was a moment before John responded. "Does Dirk have any thoughts about where Caitlyn might be? About what happened to her?"

Dylan told him everything he knew about the situation so far. "Colt and Logan are talking to Elgin Payne's grandfather now. Hopefully, he'll have some idea of where he might have taken Caitlyn."

"How certain are the authorities that Payne kidnapped her?" John's voice wavered.

"They're fairly sure, but try not to worry, Dad. Caitlyn can handle herself." Dylan closed his eyes. The muscles in his jaw bunched under the strain of not knowing what horrors might be happening to his little sister, or whether she was alive or dead.

McKenzie slid her arm around his waist and squeezed. She bent toward the phone. "John, it's McKenzie. Renegade is determined to find Caitlyn, and I have no doubt that he will. We'll be on the hunt as soon as we get a starting point, and we'll keep you posted."

"Thank you. Please keep us up to date. It's difficult being here and not knowing what's going on."

Dylan ran his palm over the back of his head. "We will. How's Ma holding up?"

"She's worried, but she's stronger than me. Always has been." Emotion swamped John's voice, and he cleared his throat. "Addison arrived this morning. She came up to stay with us while we wait to hear. She's been a comfort for your mother."

"Logan mentioned she might fly up. I'm glad she's there. I'll call again as soon as I have any news."

"Just bring your sister home."

When Dylan ended the call, McKenzie gave him an encouraging smile. "Sounds like your parents have put aside their argument, at least for now. It's good that Logan's fiancée can be with them. This must be excruciating for them."

"I didn't say anything about the wedding because knowing my mom, staying busy will help her cope. She'll probably put Addison to work, too."

"TELL us where your grandson is, Simms." Colt gripped the armrests on the chair to keep from reaching across the table and grabbing the man's shoulders to shake the answer from him.

A tick at the edge of Thomas Simms's mouth hinted at a smirk. "My grandson? How on earth would I know where he is?"

"He was seen leaving your house yesterday afternoon." Logan, who was standing, planted his palms on the Formica table-top and glowered at the older man. "Where do you think he went from there?"

"He never said anything to me about his plans."

Colt forced his hands to relax, and he leaned forward, bracing his forearms on the edge of the table. "Do you understand that if you refuse to help us, you'll add aiding and abetting a known felon, and conspiracy to commit murder after the fact, to your current charges? How well do you think you'll do in prison?"

"I can't help you if I don't know anything, gentlemen." Simms smiled beatifically.

Colt's agitation flared, and he jumped to his feet. "But you *do* know, don't you? Tell us where he is!"

Simms chuckled, and Colt shoved the table away to gain access to him. Logan grabbed him by his arm and held him back. "Colt! You're only feeding into his game.

Come on, let's get out of here. This guy isn't worth your badge, and we need to find my sister."

Colt jerked out of Logan's hold and stormed through the door. Logan followed, and they met Dylan and McKenzie outside. Dusk was deepening rapidly, and by the time they got to the car, it was fully dark. Colt phoned Dirk. "Have you found anything yet?"

"No. We talked to all the residents of the commune and searched the entire compound. No one knows anything. No one besides the boy who saw Payne. How'd you do with Simms?"

"He's not talking. Where do we go from here?"

"We'll start interviewing people in the town tomorrow. I'll start with the clerks at the grocery store. Payne might have stocked up on supplies or mentioned where he was headed. You never know."

"Tomorrow? This can't wait." Raw fear clutched Colt's throat. No way was he leaving Caitlyn with a brutal killer all night without searching for her.

Dirk's low voice dropped even deeper. "We won't get anywhere tonight."

"I'm taking Renegade out. We'll look in the forest all around the compound."

Logan rested a hand on Colt's shoulder. "We can send up drones to look for heat signatures. They can cover hundreds of miles in the time it takes us to search five."

"Yeah, but what if she's under the tree canopy?" Colt was frantic.

"Honestly," Dirk's voice vibrated through the phone, "we don't even know if she's in the forest or if Payne has her on the road headed to another town."

"We have to start somewhere," Colt pleaded. "We have to do something!"

Dylan clapped a hand on the back of Colt's neck. "I agree. We can't just sit around."

Logan nodded. "I feel as desperate as you two do, but the best thing for the dogs and for us is to get a little rest and start fresh in the morning. We'll head out before dawn. There's an APB out for the last car we know Payne was in, and the drones can pinpoint the best locations to search after sunup. We can do a pass to look for heat signatures tonight, too, but the drone will key on animal heat just as easily as human. Honestly, it will be better to use the dogs in the heavily forested areas in the morning."

Colt's hope slipped several notches. "But the longer we wait—" His phone chimed, interrupting him. Allison's number lit up the screen. He answered. "Yeah?"

"Where are you?"

"In Utah."

"Well, you just broke your first promise to Jace, and it hasn't even been forty-eight hours."

"What promise? I didn't promise him anything." His neck muscles strained under the additional stress.

"You told him you'd play ball with him after supper tonight. And you didn't even call."

Colt's shoulders drooped. "I'm sorry. It slipped my mind. I'm in Utah because Caitlyn is missing. We think she's being held by a known murderer and we're all desperately trying to find her."

Allison's voice softened. "I'm sorry to hear that, Colt. I am. But you should have called. You have to think of these things if you want to be a parent."

The truth was it hadn't crossed his mind to call. With Caitlyn missing, he'd forgotten all about playing catch. "I'm sorry, Allison. Can I talk to him?"

"No. He's already in bed. Call him tomorrow."

"I will." His shoulders ached as though he carried the world's disappointment on them. Allison ended the call, and he looked up to see his friends watching him.

Dylan asked, "That was Allison?" Colt nodded. "What did she want? Who did you want to talk to?"

"It's a long story for another day." One Colt wasn't about to tell right now. "You guys go get some rest, but I'm taking Renegade out tonight. Neither one of us is going to sleep knowing Catie is out there somewhere needing our help."

Logan grabbed his arm and pulled him around. "Listen to me, Colt. I want to be out there as much as you, but you haven't slept in almost two days. Let's take a couple of hours to rest. Renegade needs it too. He's been ramped up even longer than you. After a short two-hour nap and some food, Gunner and I will go out with you. The others can join us in the morning. We won't be any use to Caitlyn if we make stupid mistakes out of exhaustion."

Logan was right, and Colt trusted his friend's battle-forged wisdom that he'd earned in Afghanistan. Though every fiber of Colt's body yearned to press on, he took Logan's advice. "Okay. But only two hours. Then we're going out."

"Absolutely."

22

"A little discipline goes a long way. You need to learn that I can touch you whenever I want. You hear me?" Payne sneered as he raised the folded belt in his hands. He snapped it, and Caitlyn forced herself to glare at him, showing no fear. He swung the strap in the air and whipped it downward. Caitlyn curled and rolled to her side, absorbing the blow on the outer edge of her hip and thigh. She bit her lip hard, refusing to cry out. She would do everything she could to rob him of the satisfaction of her pain.

His next stroke cracked across her back and upper arm. The leather bit into her skin, the sting bringing tears to her eyes. Fury blossomed in her chest. Grinding her teeth together, she braced against three more punishing lashes—grunting in pain despite her efforts to remain silent. Hot rage fueled a fantasy of revenge.

"Don't pull away from me ever again, or next time it'll be worse." He re-threaded his belt through the loops on his jeans before he left the room, taking the light with him.

Caitlyn strained to hear if he used any secondary locks on the door. But no rattle, clank of chain, or snap of a padlock sounded from the hall. Payne was obviously confident of her restraints. With any luck, that certainty would bite him in the ass.

As soon as she was sure he'd left, Caitlyn went to work testing for any give in the ties that bound her wrists. The rough twine had rubbed her skin tender and angry. There was no play in her binds, and in the dark, she was unable to locate anything she could scrape the ropes against to cut through. She shimmied under the bed frame to feel the bolt mechanism holding the chain from her ankle to the cot. From what she could tell, it seemed that only a simple U-bolt with a mounting plate held her chain in place. The muscles in her arms burned as she strained her fingers to loosen the small nuts. She worked until her fingertips were raw and bloody, but to no avail. Eventually, her body demanded sleep, so she crawled back up onto the mattress. Rest would bring with it the renewed strength she needed to survive.

She dozed on and off, fitfully waking from nightmares of Renegade's lifeless form laying in a ditch or Colt calling out to her, but she was unable to make her voice respond in answer to him. Predawn light finally filtered in through the cloudy basement window, and Caitlyn studied the details of the room.

Sitting on the edge of the mattress, she searched for something—anything—she could scrape the rope against. A metal cabinet stood against the wall opposite her, but with the chain on her leg, it remained out of reach. The small nightstand next to the bed offered no help unless she broke it, creating a rough edge. But the sound of smashing furniture might bring Payne running. Caitlyn didn't know if he slept in the building at night. Or perhaps he left her there alone? She'd test that tonight—if she was still alive. If he went somewhere else, making noise wouldn't be a problem.

Boots clomped outside the room. Someone descended the stairs. Seconds later, a jangle clinked against the metal knob, and the door swung open. Elgin's form filled the entrance, and he held a white ceramic bowl. "Breakfast."

Thinking fast, Caitlyn responded. "I have to pee."

Payne's forehead scrunched. He'd obviously thought about feeding her, but not about her other bodily needs. This could be her chance. He set a bowl of cornflakes on the nightstand. "I'll take you after you eat."

"I can't eat cereal without my hands."

"I'll feed you."

"I really need to pee." He'd have to unlock her ankle to take her anywhere. With both legs free, she'd at least have a fighting chance.

As though he read her thoughts, Payne tilted his head. "I'll bring you a bucket." When he left, he didn't bother to close the door, so Caitlyn moved to the end of her chain, then stretching out on the floor, she peered outside the room. The door was at the bottom of a narrow staircase, and there didn't appear to be any other rooms downstairs besides the one she was in. She rolled to a sitting position as soon as she heard him at the top of the steps.

Suspicion filled his gaze when he entered the room

with a five-gallon construction bucket. "Here's your throne."

"Thanks, but I'll need my hands to—"

"I'll undo your pants." A wicked gleam lit his eyes.

"No! I'll do it myself. After you leave."

"If you gotta use the crapper bad enough, you'll do it with my help—or not at all."

Ignoring the increased speed of the throbbing in a vein at his temple, she persisted. "What about when you're not here?"

In three quick strides, he was breathing down on her. "Stand up," he commanded. When she glared at him, Payne fingered the buckle on his belt. Rather than face another beating, she pushed herself to her feet. "Good girl." He stood inches from her as he unclasped her belt. She gritted her teeth as he unbuttoned her jeans and slid down her zipper. Her body instinctively recoiled from his hands, and he laughed. "Don't move." He yanked down her pants.

Caitlyn gasped and stepped back, but she bumped up against the wall. He pushed her sideways onto the bed and tugged off her Levi's. One leg caught on her locked ankle. Payne pulled up his shirt, revealing a large scabbard strapped to his hip holding a hunting knife. He slid the knife up the trapped leg of her jeans and cut it loose in one sharp motion. "Problem solved."

He snatched the bowl from the table, spilling half the milk, and held a spoonful of soggy cereal to her mouth. She considered refusing, but her stomach growled, reminding her she needed sustenance for strength. When she finished, he held the bowl for her to drink the milk.

"Drink up. You'll need your energy for what I have planned for us this evening." He laughed, gathered up her ruined jeans, and left the room. The door slammed behind him, and she heard the metal lock click in place.

Caitlyn curled her bare legs underneath her as she sat on the edge of the bed, resolutely pushing away a growing sense of despair. She twisted her arms against the ropes that burned her raw wrists and noticed that since her jeans were no longer between the rope and her waist, there was slack in the tension.

23

_____

Under the dark sky at four in the morning, Colt and Logan drove with the dogs past Thomas Simms's house. They bounced along the uneven terrain to the hidden, homemade carport they'd found the day before. Colt toggled on the high beams. "Let's try to find the path Payne took when he drove out of here."

"It might be better if we wait until we have some daylight to see by." Logan leaned forward and peered through the windshield. "Even with the brights, I can't see more than four-feet in front of us."

"We don't have the luxury of time. Do you want to go on foot?"

"Yeah, let me and Gunner out. You follow behind shining the headlights."

Colt stopped the Expedition to let Logan and his dog out. Renegade whined to go with them. "Let him come. He's not doing any good in the car."

Colt rode the brake as he followed the ground trackers

being careful to not to drive on the worn two track drive where the car might have left tread marks. About every ten feet, Logan gestured to something he spotted in the dirt. Colt rolled down the window. "What do you see?"

"It's almost impossible to see anything with the carpet of pine straw covering the ground, but every once in a while, I think I detect tire marks in the dirt."

"Do they match the tracks under the tarp?"

"It's hard to say. We'll need forensics to tell us for sure." Logan continued his search.

The sun joined their hunt, reaching its first fingers into the forest around 5:30 a.m. Thirty minutes later, they followed the hidden drive to a paved road that presumably led to town.

Colt slammed his hand against the steering wheel. "Well, little good that did us."

"Yeah. But now we know how Payne left the compound unnoticed by Caitlyn and then caught up to her at the gas station."

"But we're back to square one. Where the hell did he take her from here?" Colt's voice rose with his panic. "They could be anywhere."

Logan opened the back door for the dogs and then climbed into the front. He rested his hand on Colt's shoulder. "We'll find her. I'm going to call Rick Sanchez, the SAC, at the FBI Office in Denver. He's gifted at figuring out the criminal mind. Maybe he can give us some insight into where this guy might go."

"It's worth a try." Disappointment flooded over Colt, and he closed his eyes. He'd hoped the tire tracks would lead someplace in the woods where he'd find Caitlyn. He was exhausted from the emotional upheaval of not knowing where she was. Not being able to help her. Not knowing if she was still alive.

Logan paced outside the car, and Colt caught bits of his side of the conversation with the Special Agent in Charge in Denver. He watched his friend run his fingers worriedly through his hair. Hair the same rich brown as Caitlyn's. Finally, Logan slid the phone from his ear and returned to the car.

"Of course, there's no guarantee, but Rick thinks it's likely that Payne will stay close to home. This is where he came when he ran, so he probably feels safe here. Rick suggests doing a drone flyover and then pinpointing search locations the drones can't see in the denser parts of the forest. He offered to come up and help us if we need him. He's a top-notch tracker, and his wife, Kendra, works with Search and Rescue K9s. They'd be a tremendous asset."

"That's awesome. If we don't find her this morning, we can call them in. Dirk assured me the Marshals have contacted local search and rescue teams to come out and hunt today too, so let's get Sanchez's thoughts to them and then get Ren and Gunner out there. If any dog can find Caitlyn in these mountains, Renegade can."

Colt drove while Logan made the calls. They passed through Tabiona and slowed at a rarely used two-track road that wound around through miles of field before it disappeared in a line of tall pine trees. "Let's see where this road goes." Colt turned onto the rough trail and took the bumps and potholes at a turtle's pace. Finally, they entered the forest canopy and were greeted by the silhouette of a grizzled man standing in the middle of the road with the morning sun at his back. He aimed a double-barreled shotgun directly at their windshield.

"Who are ya, and what d'ya want? You're trespassin' on private land." The old guy cocked his gun.

Logan raised both hands so the man could see he held no weapon before he opened his door. "I'm Special Agent Reed with the FBI. We're looking for a guy named Elgin Payne. Do you know him? His grandfather lives on the other side of town in a commune."

"You talkin' about Thomas Simms? That man is as sly as a sidewinder and just as crooked. What do you want with that no-good grandson of his?"

Logan kept his hands up and took a few steps forward, gradually approaching the man's side. "Would you mind lowering your gun? We have dogs in the car, and I'd hate to see one of them get hurt."

The man smirked and pointed the muzzle of his gun toward the ground. "What did that good-for-nothing idiot do this time?"

"He's murdered some innocent people, and now he's holding my sister," Logan gestured at Colt, "that man's fiancée, hostage. And we have to find them before he kills her, too."

Logan's words punched Colt in the gut. He knew Logan used them to jar the old hermit, but that didn't ease their impact.

"Well, he ain't been around here, nowhere." The old man worked his mouth and scratched his chin. "Seems to me that kid used to spend lots of time up inside the park. He camped up that way a lot, as I remember."

"Do you know where?" Logan glanced at Colt.

"Nah. Not exactly. But go back out to the pavement, turn right and pass the first gravel road. Take the next path you see. It's at least ten miles out and easy to miss, so keep your eyes open. That'll take you the way he used to go. Course it's a mighty big park. No telling where he went from there."

"Thanks for your help." Logan reached into his jacket pocket and the man raised his gun. "Just getting my business card. Call me if you think of anything, will you?"

"I don't have a phone, you idiot!" The man's laugh rumbled out of his chest and left him coughing. "But I'll do my best to let the sheriff know if I see anything."

Logan thanked the man, and they left. Colt cursed the twenty minutes it took them to get back out to the pavement. "Almost an hour just to talk to that old geezer."

"Yeah, but now we have a decent lead."

"Maybe. Call in our location and let's check it out."

Though Colt drove slowly, he still almost missed the turn that was hidden by overgrown shrubs on the shoulder of the highway. He barreled through the growth and took the unused track faster than he should, bouncing the Expedition's occupants without mercy. The road became rougher as they climbed in altitude, further slowing their progress. Soon, it was impassable for the large SUV, so Colt grabbed his supply pack from the back, and they struck out on foot. The mountain scenery would have been awe-inspiring if Colt's total focus wasn't on finding Caitlyn.

Miles later, they rounded a bend and came to a ledge, offering a stunning view of the valley below. When the team of four paused to catch their breath, Colt saw a flash of sunlight glinting off something inside a grove of dense vegetation about a mile away. He squinted to see what caused the reflection in the mid-day sun. "Logan, look! Is that a car?"

"Could be!" Logan held up his binoculars. "It's a car alright. Let's hope it's the one we're looking for!" He took off running across the field toward the stand of trees. "Gunner, Renegade, *kemne*!"

24

Caitlyn didn't know when Payne would return, but she didn't hear him moving upstairs, so she assumed he had left. Ignoring the burning skin around her wrists, she worked frantically at the knots holding her arms to her waist. Telling herself to calm down and breathe, she tried again. If possible, she wanted to be ready to attack Payne when he returned. So far, she'd only received a whipping from him, but he was keeping her alive for a reason. A reason she didn't allow her mind to linger on for too long. Escape meant survival, and that's what she focused on.

She dug at the tight knots, ripping her fingernails below the skin. If only she could reach the rope with her teeth.

Mid-day came and went. Apparently, Payne didn't think she needed lunch, but the limp cornflakes hadn't lasted long, and her stomach complained. Her throat was dry too, and her lips cracked, but still she worked on the knots.

Late in the day, it occurred to her that Payne might not come back. What if he got into a car accident or just left her there to die? She'd had a little water today, but without more, she'd only last three or four more days. Five tops. Caitlyn shook her head. "Focus, Caitlyn. Those kinds of thoughts will not get you out of here," she spoke the words aloud to herself.

The rope loosened. Caitlyn froze and held her breath. *Did it really slide?* She pulled again, and it slackened more! Hinges squeaked somewhere overhead. Payne was back. She had only seconds.

His loud clomping footfalls stomped down the stairs. The lock clicked, and the door opened. Payne held a paper bag with spreading grease spots in one hand and a beer can in the other. The room filled with the tantalizing aroma of fried chicken. Caitlyn's stomach rolled over itself, and her mouth watered. Elgin's eyes were glassy and wild. He was drunk. This was not good.

"There you are, all nice and waiting for me on the bed." He laughed and lunged at her. Caitlyn flinched but was careful to keep her hands at her waist. "If you're a good girl, I might share my supper. After." He set the bag and the beer on the nightstand and stared hungrily down at her.

Caitlyn bided her time, watching for him to make the first move. "Maybe you should unlock my ankle. It might make things more comfortable."

His harsh laugh barked at her. "I don't care if you're comfortable, and it turns me on having you all tied up." He sat on the edge of the bed and ran his hand up her bare thigh. Her skin puckered in disgust. She breathed in and waited.

He reached for his beer, turning his back to her. This was her chance! Perhaps the only one she'd get. Caitlyn sprang. She had freed her hands from the tether at her waist, but they were still bound together. Looping her hands over his head, she stretched the rope taught across the front of his neck. She pulled back with all her might.

Payne roared like a wounded beast. He spun, but she clung to his shoulders, wrapping her free leg around his body. He clawed at her arms. She held fast. Rising to his feet, he rammed her back against the wall. Every ounce of breath burst from her lungs. But her will to survive was greater than the agony of refilling her stunned chest. He reached for her hair and yanked. Her scalp ignited.

Pain fueled her rage, but she remembered her training. Breathing, she forced her mind into clarity. Her adversary was bigger and stronger than she was, and she would use that to her advantage. Caitlyn pulled harder against his throat, surprised at how long it took for him to lose consciousness. He threw his head back to smash into her face, but she was ready. She turned away, the blow glancing off her temple. Her wrists screamed.

The furious man bucked and writhed, reminding Caitlyn of bronc-riding when she was younger. If she could stay on a 1300-pound horse that was determined to throw her, she could hold on to this monster. She gripped him tighter with her arms and legs, the shackle cutting into her ankle. He tore at her flesh and swung to the side, but he stumbled. He was losing the battle. His brain needed oxygen that she didn't allow. He dropped to one knee. Caitlyn pulled tighter. He slumped to the floor, and still she held.

Caitlyn waited until his body was completely still for several seconds before she slid off his back. Rolling him over, she searched his pockets for the keys. It was challenging to get them out of his pants with bleeding fingertips and her hands tied together, but she finally retrieved them. Fumbling, she found the key for the lock on her ankle.

She freed her foot, and the thick shackle fell, hitting Elgin's hand. He groaned. He was alive and quickly waking. Caitlyn had no time to waste. She lifted the small bedside table high and smashed it over Payne's head, then ran out the door. She sprinted up the stairs, but as she reached the top, she heard him moving below. There was no time to look for her pants or shoes. The stairway opened to a small shack. She glanced around and grabbed a few items that might help her—a length of rope, a canvas tarp, and what looked like a bag of hand tools.

Bursting through the door, she ran as fast as she could for the cover of the surrounding forest. Sharp sticks, thistles, and stones tore at her bare feet and legs as she raced away. She had barely ducked into the trees when Payne burst from the shack and roared. His fury echoed between the mountains, and Caitlyn sprinted faster. She leapt over a log but landed wrong on the other side of it. Rolling her ankle, she fell to her knees. On her way down, she clapped her hand over her mouth to prevent herself from crying out and giving away her location. Pain shot fiery jolts up her leg as she gripped onto her injured joint. But she had to keep moving.

25

Colt and Logan ran with the dogs to the abandoned car, and after Logan offered the sweatshirt with Caitlyn's scent to them, he commanded them to search. Colt watched Renegade for any sign that he smelled Caitlyn's trail. Both dogs alerted at the sedan, and Logan opened the driver's door to search inside. Colt rummaged through the passenger's side. He unlatched the glove box and sucked in a breath.

Logan gave him a sharp glance. "What is it?"

"Catie's badge and gun." The sight of those particular items flattened Colt somehow, but he snapped around when Logan commanded the dogs.

"*Stopa*! Find her, boys!" Logan kept Gunner on his leash but let Renegade search freely.

Colt stuffed Caitlyn's things into his pack while Logan managed the dogs. Caitlyn's brother led Gunner in a spiral from the car outward. His dog quickly caught a scent and left the spiral to follow his nose. Renegade ran a serpentine over the same odor trail and took off, bounding far ahead of them all.

Colt's blood spiked with adrenaline. "Come on, Logan. This way!"

Logan held onto Gunner's leash, but nothing was going to hold Caitlyn's dog back from an all-out sprint. They followed an overgrown path into the woods. Renegade came to a stream and lapped up several mouthfuls of water as he ran through it, but hesitated on the other side to sniff the bank. He'd lost the scent, but without being told, began another serpentine search.

"Damn it!" Colt's heart thudded against his rib cage.

Logan pulled up beside him. "Don't worry, he'll pick her scent up again."

"What if Payne made her walk through the water? Who knows which direction they went?" Panic threatened. He'd felt so close a minute ago and now had to fight off desperation.

"We'll send the dogs in opposite directions. When one of them finds her trail again, we'll go from there. You follow Ren."

Colt splashed through the cold mountain water to the far side of the stream and pointed to his left. "Find her, Renegade. Find Catie!" Renegade took off in the direction Colt indicated, with his nose to the ground, swerving back and forth. Logan and Gunner ran the other way.

After they'd gone about a half a mile, Gunner's barks echoed through the trees, and Logan gave a sharp whistle. Both Colt and Renegade turned around and ran toward them. Motioning with his arms, Logan shouted, "Gunn's got her scent! Let's go!"

They searched all day. Drones flew overhead, peering down from a bird's-eye view until dusk settled in the valley. After tracking all afternoon and into the evening through the thick woods, the forest finally opened to a clearing. The men and dogs paused at the edge of the tree line to catch their breath.

Logan sucked water from a bottle he carried on his hip and offered some to Colt. "Put Ren's leash on. We can't afford to let him run free and get hurt this far away from civilization."

Colt clipped Renegade's leash to his harness while Logan pinged their location to the search headquarters in Tabiona and also to Dylan's phone and sent everyone a text.

Logan: **Dogs are on Caitlyn's trail. Getting dark. Send backup to these coordinates.**

Dirk texted back: **On it. Gold and I are bringing a team your way.**

Colt reached into his pack. After tossing Logan an energy bar and opening his own, he studied the clearing through his field binoculars. "It's getting too dark to see."

CAITLYN ESTIMATED she had covered about five miles. Considering that even with a sprained ankle, she was in much better shape than Payne—and the fact that she'd denied his brain of oxygen causing him to lose consciousness—she trusted she had enough time to find shelter to hide in and tend to her wounds. Darkness descended, and if she found a good spot, the lack of light would be a blessing.

Her ankle was badly sprained, and pain stabbed like a red-hot poker with each step. Running through the pain had certainly worsened the situation, but she had no choice. The joint was hot and purple. It was so swollen she could no longer see or feel her ankle bone. But she continued to limp along anyway, doing her damnedest to ignore the agony.

Finding herself at the base of a cliff wall, she searched for cover and finally found it behind a thick grouping of wild raspberry bushes. Granite surrounded the niche on all sides, except for the opening she crawled through, so neither Payne nor any hungry forest animal could sneak up on her in the night. Prickly raspberry thorns scratched and stung her bare skin as she pushed behind the bushes. Caitlyn fought tears of pain and exhaustion.

Once she settled in, Caitlyn plucked a handful of berries and greedily crammed them in her mouth. While she chewed, she unzipped the bag she'd grabbed from the shack. It proved to be a goldmine. It carried an assortment of tools, many of which couldn't help her. But at the bottom of the pouch, she discovered a hunting knife. Overcome with relief, tears swelled again, this time flooding over her eyelids. She waited for them to recede, and as soon as she could see again, she dug a shallow hole to bury the bag.

Quickly, she held the knife between her knees and cut the rope from her bleeding wrists. She shook out her arms and blew on the burned skin. Using the blade again, she cut strips from the tarp and wrapped her twisted ankle. The pressure helped to relieve the pain instantly. She fashioned more wraps for her cut and bruised feet, tying them on with pieces of the rope. Finally, she draped the remainder of the canvas around her body and tied it at her waist to protect her bare legs.

With her foot propped up on a nearby rock, Caitlyn rested back and closed her eyes. She wouldn't sleep, but even a few minutes of rest would help. Stars sparkled overhead, brilliantly bright, and she wished she had learned how to navigate by them. The boys—Colt and her brothers—had mastered the skill in boy scouts, but she stubbornly refused to let them teach her since girls weren't allowed to join the club. Her pride had always been her downfall.

She must have dozed for a few seconds, or minutes, because she woke at the snap of a twig.

26

Renegade pulled hard on the leash attached to his vest as he followed his nose. It was all Colt could do to hang on. A serene mountain meadow opened up before them, carpeting the flat expanse between two mountain ranges with tall grass and summer flowers. The men crashed into the peaceful scenery following the dogs toward the distant trees across the expanse.

Logan pulled up, breathing hard. "Look at this flattened grass. What would cause that, do you think?" He gestured at a long stretch of flat foliage about three feet wide that stretched out before them.

"Hard to say," Colt panted. "But the dogs are headed along its length. Let's go." He pointed in the direction they had been going. "Find her, Ren!"

Renegade barked excitedly and took off, jerking Colt's arm as he pumped his legs to keep up. Caitlyn's dog pulled him along around a peninsula of trees to their left. In the center of a new open stretch stood an old, gray shack.

"Logan!" Colt yelled. Renewed energy surged through Colt's limbs as he and Renegade sprinted toward the lone building.

The flattened grass path they had been following led to the weathered structure. Rolled up and tucked next to the shed was a quarter-inch thick sheet of heavy plastic with handles attached to one side. Someone must have used it like a sled to drag something... or someone... to the hut.

Renegade was the first to arrive, barking fiercely. He rammed into the door, scratching at the old wood with his claws.

A few seconds later, Logan and Gunner ran up behind the dogs. Colt slid his sidearm out of its holster and he waited for Logan to do the same. The men took up positions on either side of the flimsy door.

"I'm going in." Colt reached for the door and yanked it open. No sound came from within. Holding his weapon and a flashlight pointed toward the ground, he stepped sideways across the threshold, leveled his gun, and cleared the room. Logan repeated the maneuver, bringing the dogs with him. The room they entered was small and mostly empty. Several buckets sat stacked under the window next to a broken chair. A few fishing poles leaned against the wall in the corner. Thick dust covered the room and its contents.

"This is probably somebody's hunting or fishing shack. Looks like some old tools and just a bunch of junk." Logan studied the variety of items on a makeshift tool bench.

Renegade sniffed the seam at the bottom of a second door and barked frantically as he clawed at the wood of what looked to be a closet or storage space. From Renegade's strong reaction, Caitlyn was probably inside the closet, and Colt hesitated a fraction of a second before he reached for the knob, bracing for what he might find on the other side. Logan took a position next to the opening, holding his Glock in both hands and looking ready for horror.

Colt's stomach cramped as he opened the door. He released a huge breath when he saw a staircase leading below ground. Logan gestured for him to continue down the stairs. A splintered door, torn from its hinges, lay across the lower landing at the bottom of the steps. Colt called, "Catie?"

Colt unclipped the leash, and Renegade bounded down the steps. He sprang over the broken door, disappearing into a darkened room. Colt ran after him. He tilted the obstacle out of his way and he and Logan followed with Gunner at Logan's heel. Logan brightened the room with the flashlight from his utility belt, sending its beam into each of the shadowy corners. "She's not here."

"But she was." Colt lifted a thick chain with an ankle shackle welded to the end. He fell back against the cold wall, desperately working to steady his breath and get a handle on his fear. When Logan's light panned across the floor, Colt noticed the cut-up jeans and pair of panties by the side of the bed. A jolt of pain speared his chest. Dear God, what had happened in here? Where was Catie, and what was she going through? Colt pictured her curled into a ball, scared and abused. Breath-steeling rage replaced his fear, and he released a roar of agonized frustration.

"Colt!" Logan grabbed hold of his shoulders and shook him hard. "The fact that Payne held Caitlyn here is a good sign. If he wanted to kill her, she'd already be dead. He has other plans, which means she has a chance—and so do we. Now, let's go find her!" He ran out of the room, calling, "Gunner!"

But Renegade beat all of them up the stairs and, untethered, bolted outside. The sun had plunged below the horizon, leaving only twilight. Logan paused long enough to send Dirk and Dylan their current coordinates and to tell him what they had found.

Colt flew past Logan and chased after Renegade, who ran in an all-out sprint. The dog's stride spanning a good twelve feet. There was no way the men could keep up with Renegade, but Colt knew the dog was on Caitlyn's trail as Ren flew through the dusk toward a black silhouette of trees.

REACHING her fingers into the foliage that hid her position, Caitlyn peeked out through the raspberry leaves, and a cold wash of relief poured through her veins. A fat raccoon perched on a rotted log, and munched on something in his little hands. Caitlyn's muscles relaxed as she laughed silently at herself. She was thankful for the little sleep she'd had, but it was time to move. A hot spike of pain seared her ankle when she stood. Knowing her injury would slow her down,

Caitlyn looked around for a way to slow Payne down, too.

The moon glistened off the white canvas she'd tied around her waist, so she quickly rubbed soil and crushed leaves into the fabric to serve as camouflage. While she was at it, she spit into a handful of dirt and rubbed the grit over her face, before sticking twigs and pine needles into her hair for further cover.

Limping, Caitlyn moved to the edge of the rock face. When the granite ended, she crawled on the ground, searching for a thick stick sturdy enough to use as a crutch. Along the way, she gathered smaller, half-inch sticks to make a booby-trap. She'd never outrun Payne with her sprained ankle, but she'd be ready for him if he found her.

Aiming toward the sound of flowing water, Caitlyn ambled over the rough mountain terrain to what she hoped was a river. Her footing gave way, and she stumbled. Falling, she bounced and rolled down the side of an eroded bank toward the water. Tree branches whipped against her arms and cheeks. She landed in a crumpled heap at the bottom of the slope, face first in an ice-cold stream. After sucking in a shocked breath, she leaned back and lapped up mouthfuls of the crisp water, vaguely hoping it was clean enough to drink without making her sick.

Dawn rolled up on the edge of the night sky, giving her enough dim light to see that she'd left an obvious path where she'd skidded and fallen down the hill. She rested against a large stone while she whittled the ends of her gathered sticks into sharp points. Dipping her foot in and out of the frigid water, she soaked her swollen joint as she reviewed her survival strategy.

With another strip cut from the edge of the tarp, she lashed the carved darts onto a flexible tree branch. When she was finished, the sharp sticks jutted out perpendicular to the bough. She then tied the dart-studded branch backward, with a long string she'd pulled from the canvas weave. Wrapping the string around the trunk and pulling it taught across the path, she fashioned a makeshift tripwire an inch above the ground. She secured the string on the opposite side of the path with a stone to maintain its tension. Satisfied, she covered it with dirt and pine needles to hide the trap.

If Payne followed her down the hill, he'd stumble on the string and release the branch armed with spears. The bough would whip back across the path and into his legs. Though the wounds he'd suffer wouldn't be enough to stop him, they would certainly slow him down.

Rushing to beat the sun, Caitlyn hobbled downward along the bank of the stream. Her dad always taught her, if she ever got lost, to follow any water downhill. People and towns gather at the water. It was her best bet. If she was going to survive this, she needed help.

Caitlyn had hobbled about a mile when she heard a man's scream bounce off the mountain walls behind her. *Payne!* He must have tripped the dart trap. She increased her pace, though her ankle burned. Ahead, a rock outcropping loomed over the stream. If she could get to it before he found her, she could hide.

The morning sun had already heated the stone, and she warmed her aching hands on the rough surface. The icy water had eased her swollen joint, but the rest of her body shivered with the cold. Caitlyn pulled herself up onto the rocks and leaned back below the upper edges of the grouping to hide herself from the man who hunted her. He wasn't far behind.

She rested her head on the stony pillow and stretched out her legs. Her bare skin was bruised and scraped. She brushed dirt away from a skinned spot on her knee, but her every muscle froze when she heard a rattle. A snake!

Caitlyn didn't move. Didn't breathe. She tried to judge where the angry serpent was coiled. The knife she carried was below her right hip, but if she moved for it, the venomous reptile would surely strike. Hopefully, if she lay completely still, the snake would settle down and slither away. Caitlyn's skin crawled despite her resolve not to react.

On the other side of her stone hiding place, she heard Payne's arrival. He huffed and moaned with each heavy step of his injured leg. "When I find you, Deputy... and I will find you... I'm going to choke the life out of you, nice and slow! I'm gonna watch the light leave your damned eyes." He was close enough for Caitlyn to hear his mumbling, and her muscles tensed reflexively. The rattle intensified, and Caitlyn's survival instinct clamored through her nervous system.

Payne's shadow appeared across her legs, and her body jerked involuntarily. The snake struck, clamping its fangs into her bare calf. She screamed in pain; her knife already flying through the air, she deftly decapitated the serpent. She pulled its fangs from her leg, leaving two bloody punctures, and tossed the terrifying head into the water.

Giving her no time to recover or think, Payne sprang on her. His eyes were wild in his grimacing face. Caitlyn screamed again, seconds before he clamped down on her throat with his large, vice-like hands. He squeezed hard, cutting off both her breath and the blood flow to her brain. She had seconds before she lost consciousness.

With pure adrenaline-powered survival instinct, Caitlyn swung her arm around and plunged the knife she held into her attacker's side. He roared and reared back, giving her a little space to move. Her head swam, but she sucked in a breath and the with what little strength she had remaining, she forced the blade inward and up. Dark blood gushed from his wound, covering her hand and body with a warm, sticky gore. As he collapsed on top of her, a look of surprise passed through his eyes. He stared down at what they both knew was a fatal wound.

To be certain, Caitlyn rammed the knife tip an inch farther up and pierced his lung. Payne rolled back in shock. Blood trickled from the corner of his mouth, and he looked at her in confusion. She tried to scramble away, but he caught her arm in his meaty fist.

COLT CALLED OUT TO RENEGADE, and the dog paused for him to catch up. He clipped the leash onto Ren's vest. It had grown too dark to see more than shades of black and gray in the deep forest. The lack of light slowed Colt down, if not the dog, and they had to adjust to the limitation. Colt held his flashlight, but he hesitated to use it, not wanting to give away his presence.

"Good boy, Ren. We'll find her. Keep going!" He spoke quietly into Renegade's neck. The dog pulled him along, and Colt did his best not to trip. Gunner and Logan were somewhere behind them. Colt hadn't waited while Logan stayed back to search the building. He was as desperate as Renegade to get to Caitlyn, and Gunner would easily track them when Logan was ready to follow. They ran through the night, taking only momentary breaks for Colt to catch his breath.

When the morning sun stretched its arms into the sky, Colt—though beyond exhaustion—ran faster. At his next breath-catching pause, he released Renegade from his tether. Ren had to be worn out too, but not waiting for Colt, the dog took off. He paused at the rim of a drop-off, and then ran down the slope. Colt bolted after him.

The scuffed earth on the incline was raw, and the steep bank ended at the edge of a stream below. The dirt was moist, so Colt knew they weren't far behind Caitlyn. Obviously, more than one person had skidded down this hill. That meant Payne was still chasing her too. Colt forced his legs to move faster against his fatigue. At the bottom of the hill, Renegade sniffed at a tree branch lashed with sharp, blood-covered sticks. Colt's gut dissolved to into liquid. *Oh, God—Catie!*

Renegade sprang past the bloody trap, into the water beyond. He leapt onto the opposite bank and, with his nose to the ground, ran along the edge of the stream. A piercing scream stopped Colt's heart from beating. His body jolted to a halt for half a breath and then, surging with renewed protective energy, he blasted through the trees toward the sound.

From a distance, Colt heard Renegade barking and snarling, and then there was silence. Colt's boots pounded the ground underneath him as he flew in the direction the sounds had come from. He burst through the trees and there she was!

Caitlyn, wrapped in a tarp and covered in blood, tumbled down a pile of rocks. Renegade stood atop the outcropping. His jaws were locked onto a man's throat. Blood spilled down the rock face. Colt dashed to Caitlyn and gathered her in his arms. "Catie! Thank God! We found you—we're here. You're safe now! Are you shot? Where are you hurt?" He tore the canvas sheet away from her body, searching for wounds.

"Colt! Thank, God!" Caitlyn dissolved into tears, smearing dirt across her face as she wiped at them. "I knew you'd come."

When Payne no longer moved, Renegade left his still body and bounded down the rocks to Caitlyn's side. He slathered her face with his tongue.

"Are you bleeding?" Colt continued to check her for injuries.

"No… but…" Her words slowed. "Ren," she breathed. "I thought Payne killed him! But, I knew you would come for me."

Colt noticed her purple ankle just before he saw the two parallel puncture marks on her calf. "Is that a snake bite?" He searched Caitlyn's eyes, but they blinked closed. She clutched his arms, but then her body went limp. "Caitlyn!"

27

Caitlyn woke to find herself on a white-sheeted bed, connected to tubes and monitors. Colt stood with his back to the room talking on the phone, while Dirk and her brothers hovered at the foot of her bed, speaking in hushed tones. McKenzie sat on a chair next to the bed, holding her hand.

"Where's Ren?" Caitlyn's throat was raw and dry.

McKenzie smiled. "Guys, Caitlyn's awake."

The men all turned to face her, and she heard Colt say, "Jace, I've got to go. Caitlyn just woke up. I'll call you as soon as we get back to Moose Creek." He ended the call and rushed to the side of Caitlyn's bed opposite McKenzie. Lifting her cold hand with his warm one, he said, "Hey, tough guy. How're you feeling?"

"I'm not sure." Caitlyn blinked. "Good, I guess. Am I on painkillers?" Her mind seemed kind of cloudy, but not dull. She ran a quick physical inventory of her body and was rewarded with a sharp pain when she wiggled her toes. "I think my ankle is sprained, but other than some scrapes, bruises, and a snake bite, I should be fine in a few minutes."

Colt shook his head and chuffed. "I think it'll be a little longer than a few minutes. The doc says you have to stay in the hospital for rest and rehydration for at least 24 hours, and you've been given anti-venom for the snake bite, but they want to monitor your leg."

Caitlyn opened her mouth to speak, but Logan interrupted her. "Don't try to argue, Catie-did. You're not going anywhere. Besides, I've arranged for you guys to catch a ride home with me and Gunner on an FBI helicopter on its way back to Denver. And that won't happen until tomorrow afternoon, anyway."

Caitlyn looked from Logan to Colt. "But what about my truck? I need to drive it home."

"Not happening." Colt pulled a chair close to her bed and sat. "Besides, Renegade tore your truck interior to shreds trying to get out to help you when Payne abducted you."

"Oh, no!" Caitlyn glanced around the room again. "Where is Ren? Why isn't he here?"

Logan tapped her blanket-covered toe. "He's with Gunner. Mara took them to a dog park to let them run off some energy. They'll be back soon."

"I can't believe I let Payne sneak up on me like that."

Colt's cheeks turned ruddy. "It was my fault. We were arguing."

"No." Caitlyn shook her head. "Still, he shouldn't have been able to incapacitate me."

Sitting on the edge of her bed, Dylan said, "The doctor

thinks Payne probably covered your nose and mouth with a chloroform saturated cloth."

That gave her some solace regarding her self-defense skills. "Poor Renegade. It's no wonder he went crazy. And then, he saved my life. Again. I owe that dog everything." She brought Colt's hand to her lips and kissed his knuckles. "And you, too. What would I do without you coming to my rescue?"

"We didn't rescue you, Catie. You saved yourself. All we did was find you in time to get you to the hospital before the snake venom spread through your bloodstream."

"But you guys found me. I knew you would." Her eyelids, suddenly heavy, drooped. "Where is Payne? Did he survive?"

Colt shook his head. "No."

Changing the subject, Logan said, "You've done a great job with Renegade, Caitlyn, that's for sure." His eyes gleamed with pride. "He's the one who found you."

"He's the best dog, ever." Caitlyn blinked, fighting the sleep that pressed on her.

McKenzie moved to stand next to Dylan, and Dirk took the seat she left next to Caitlyn. "I'll get your truck home for you, Reed. You just worry about getting back on your feet. Got it?"

"Yes, sir." Caitlyn smiled at him. "Thanks."

"Don't thank me yet. I'm not sure that beat-up hunk of junk will make it all the way back to Wyoming."

"Sure, it will." She smirked before her eyes closed and her mind floated away on a cloud.

THE FBI'S BELL 407 helicopter landed in the pasture behind the red barn at Reed Ranch, its huge propellers flattening the grass to the ground under its powerful gusts. Both dogs leapt out the door and were followed by Caitlyn's brothers. Logan called the dogs away from the rotors, and Dylan helped McKenzie out.

Caitlyn's dad had driven his pickup down to the field to meet them, and Colt carried her from the helicopter, laying her in the back seat of the truck.

"You gave us quite a scare, young lady." Her dad tried to glower at her, but she could see the love and relief filling his eyes.

"I know. I'm sorry, Dad."

He bent over and kissed her forehead, pressing his lips against her skin for a long moment.

When everyone was clear, the helicopter rotors picked up speed. They all waved to the pilots as the midnight-blue craft lifted off the ground, then everyone climbed into the truck bed, and Caitlyn's dad drove them up to the house. Stella, followed by Addison, ran toward the truck and yanked open the back door. "Caitlyn Reed, don't you ever scare me like that again!" Her mother kissed her several times on the face.

"I'm sorry, Mama. I'll try not to."

"Let's get you into bed. Colt?" her mother directed.

"No, Mom. I don't want to go to bed. I'll just rest on the couch, okay?"

Dylan helped Colt slide Caitlyn out of the truck.

236

"Can't stand not to be in the middle of everything, can you?" Her brother winked and shook his head at her.

"Somebody has to keep an eye on you guys." Caitlyn's heart overflowed with love for the people gathered around her. These people mattered more than anything. They were the reason she did what she did—to make the world a safer place for them.

After Colt had settled her on the couch and covered her with a quilt, her mom served a simple meal of tomato soup and grilled cheese sandwiches. Before long, Logan and Addison got ready to leave. "We'll be back before you know it. Dylan and McKenzie's wedding is in less than two weeks."

"I wish you'd just stay." Their mom gave Logan a kiss on the cheek.

"I wish we could, Ma. But we have to get back to work." Logan hugged their mother.

Addison did the same and waved before they left through the kitchen to collect Gunner from the backyard. They let Renegade inside and he scampered in to take up his guard position next to the couch. Caitlyn reached over and scratched his soft ears. Her eyes closed, and she fell into the alluring arms of sleep.

28

The following morning, after a breakfast fit for King Solomon himself, of eggs, bacon, sausage, pancakes, and fresh fruit, Caitlyn crutched her way out to the backyard to watch the Belgian puppies play, the sun gleaming off their silky, mahogany coats. She sat at the picnic table and propped her injured leg on the bench while Renegade lay in the grass and rested his chin on top of her good foot. Bear gnawed on a stick twice his size in the shade while the new litter grew tired and crowded at Athena's belly to nurse and doze.

Caitlyn thought about McKenzie's proposal to breed Athena and Renegade. Maybe it was a good idea. After all, Renegade was the best dog in the world, so having a bunch of puppies like him had to be a wise plan. She lazily stroked the sleek fur on the top of his head. She owed her life to him. How did she get so lucky with a rescue dog?

Colt had texted her earlier that he'd be there around ten as soon as he met with Wes and set their plans for the day. Laurie Dillinger had called too. She and Caleb were driving down from Montana to pick up Bear. It would be good to see them. Caitlyn hoped they were coping alright after Sam's recent death. She couldn't imagine how difficult it must be for them. A wave of grief washed through her heart at the memory of her friend and partner. She held her breath and waited for the ache in her chest to pass.

The Moose Creek Sheriff's Jeep rolled to a stop near the back gate, and Colt got out and waved. She smiled back, wondering who else was in the car. The passenger door opened and Colt's mini-me climbed out. Caitlyn drew in a deep breath and kept her smile pasted to her mouth.

They approached the fence, and Colt rested his hand on the back of the boy's neck. "How's the patient?" Colt asked as he unlatched the gate.

Caitlyn couldn't help staring at the boy. It was so strange to see the two of them side-by-side like this. "I'll live," she answered.

Jace approached her cautiously and peered at her leg. "Did you *really* get bit by a rattler?"

She couldn't repress the grin that came in response to his boyish interest. Colt checked Jace's behavior, though. "You should probably introduce yourself before you start staring at Catie's injuries and asking a bunch of questions."

Jace looked up at her, unapologetically. "Hi. I'm Jace. So, what did it feel like?"

Caitlyn laughed despite herself. "Just a quick, sharp jab. It happened so fast, it's hard to remember."

The boy's eyes widened in wonder. "Then you

chopped off its head?"

Caitlyn crunched her brows together and stared up at Colt in question.

He laughed. "Well—you *did*."

"That's so awesome!" Jace reached out as if to touch her leg and then drew his hand back sheepishly.

Caitlyn pursed her lips to keep from laughing. "You want to see the bite, don't you?"

Jace nodded. So, she pulled up the tape and folded the bandage back for him to see. She didn't think it was all that impressive. Only two red-black puncture wounds from the fangs and a swollen purple and green bruise.

"Wow! That's super cool." The boy blinked up at her. "I bet it hurt."

"Yeah, I wouldn't want to do it again," Caitlyn agreed. Jace's attention shifted then to the puppies, and he dashed off to investigate. "He's really cute, Colt."

Colt leaned down to kiss her, then he stuffed his hands in his pants pockets. "He's a great kid. I wanted you to meet him. I thought I'd introduce him to your folks too if they're around."

"My mom's in the kitchen and my dad—"

"Is right here." Her dad stepped out onto the back porch and watched Jace play with the puppies. Colt seemed to hold his breath; his eyes glued to her dad. Caitlyn slid her hand into his and squeezed.

"Jace, come over and meet Mr. Reed," Colt called.

The boy looked up, and obviously torn between minding his manners and staying with the puppies, he reluctantly walked up to Caitlyn's dad and held out his hand. "Hi, Mr. Reed. I'm Jace." Caitlyn wondered if Colt practiced introductions with his son before they came.

Her dad took the little hand in his. "Nice to meet you, Jace. How about the two of us get started on the right foot? Since Colt and Caitlyn are going to be married, that makes me kind of a grandpa to you. Would you like to call me Grandpa John?"

Jace tilted his head and, closing one eye, peered up at the older man. "Well, my mom's dad is called Grandpa Allen. How 'bout I call you Papa John?"

Caitlyn's mouth dropped open. How was it that easy for her dad to slide into the boy's life? She glanced up to see what Colt thought of the scene and, in that moment, witnessed raw love and admiration brimming in his eyes for her father. Her heart overflowed.

Her mom stepped out of the kitchen onto the back porch, carrying a tray with a pitcher of lemonade, glasses, and a plate of sugar cookies. "Anyone thirsty?" She smiled down at Jace. "Hello. I'm Stella, Caitlyn's mom. You look like you could use a drink."

"Yes, please!" Jace jumped off the porch steps and ran to take a seat across from Caitlyn at the picnic table. He was an endearing boy, and Caitlyn wondered if she'd ever get used to how much he looked like Colt had when he was ten. It was like she had fallen back through a looking glass of time.

Renegade got up, and after stretching and shaking out his tawny coat, he wandered over to Jace and sniffed him. His cold nose made Jace squeal with laughter.

"Colt, will you and Jace be staying for lunch?" Stella asked. "I thought we could grill some hotdogs?"

"Sure, that'd be great. I have him for the day, and I thought he'd like to see the ranch and meet everyone. Plus, I figured he'd love seeing the puppies and the horses."

Caitlyn swung her leg down and pushed her crutch aside to make room for the others. "Laurie and Caleb are coming down to get Bear after lunch."

Colt's brow creased. "I can't think of anything that will help that little fella get through the next few years better than Bear." Colt sat next to her, kissed her cheek, and whispered, "It's okay with you that I brought Jace out for the day, isn't it?"

Caitlyn's chest was heavy with an emotion she couldn't decipher, but she pushed it aside. "Of course. He's always welcome here. This is practically your home, too."

After they'd finished lunch, Laurie and Caleb arrived. They drove into the barnyard and parked beside Colt's Jeep. As soon as she unlatched Caleb's car seat, the little boy jumped down and ran through the gate in search of Bear. When he saw his puppy, he dove onto the lawn near the black and tan bundle, and they cavorted together in the grass.

Jace left his spot next to the Malinois pups and sat on his knees near Caleb. The boys played together with the Rottweiler puppy as though they'd known each other all their lives, while the grownups sat in the shade, sipped lemonade, nibbled cookies, and caught up with each other.

"Caleb seems to be doing well, Laurie, but how are you?" Caitlyn asked.

Laurie shrugged and wiped the condensation off her glass with a napkin. "I get up every morning. Some days, that's my greatest accomplishment."

Caitlyn reached for her hand. "I bet even that's hard on a lot of days. Do you need anything? Can I help in any way?"

Her friend gave her a wry look. "You can try to be more careful. You could have been killed, Caitlyn. I couldn't deal with that."

Caitlyn shifted her gaze to Colt, who glanced away. "It was a freak thing."

"So was the bomb that killed Sam. Why is it that all of you choose to have such dangerous jobs?"

Caitlyn didn't answer right away, and when she did, it was barely more than a whisper. "I want to make the world a safer place. I know Sam felt the same way."

Laurie sighed. "I know, and you are making it safer. I'm sorry. I shouldn't have said that. It's just…"

"I understand." Caitlyn hugged her friend.

Jace helped Caleb play tug-of-war with Bear and the stick, and while they pulled, he said, "Colt told me your dad died."

Caitlyn sat upright and Colt stood, but Caleb didn't seem to mind, and he answered matter of fact, "Yeah, he did. I really miss him."

Jace nodded and slid his arm around Caleb's chubby middle. "My dad died too. I bet he would have liked your puppy."

"My dad would have loved him." The boys stood side-by-side, watching Bear drag the stick behind him through the grass.

"Come on." Jace tugged Caleb's arm. "Let's go see the new puppies. We can name them." And just like that, the heavy moment broke into sunshine and the boys took off, running together toward Athena's whelping box, leaving the adults gawking and speechless.

Soon, a broad smile stretched across Caitlyn's mouth. She appreciated Jace's direct, no-nonsense nature, and she decided they were going to get along just fine.

Colt was watching her. He smiled and sat down next to her. "Jace's approach reminds me of yours."

She chuckled. "You'll have to teach him the art of polite conversation then. It sure isn't my forte, that's the truth."

A soft smile graced Laurie's face as she observed her son and his new friend. "Caitlyn, your straightforwardness was one of the traits Sam admired about you the most."

Colt's phone buzzed, and he checked the screen. He swiped and answered. After a short conversation, he returned his phone to his pocket. "That was the sheriff up in Billings. Tito Garza's ready to talk. He wants to make a deal."

"That's great news." Caitlyn's pulse leapt.

"But he says he'll only talk to you."

Caitlyn drew her brows together. "Me? Why?"

"He claims he felt a connection with you the day he came down to Moose Creek to identify his wife's body."

Caitlyn sat taller. "Okay, then. When do we go?"

29

The next day, Colt and Caitlyn sat side-by-side in the hard chairs at the table in the Billings Police Department. They waited silently for Tito Garza to join them in the interview room. When the guard finally escorted Garza in, Colt was shocked by his unkempt appearance. Garza's usual robust pallor was gray, and his dark eyes seemed to have sunken in. His perfectly trimmed and combed hair was mussed and hung in his face.

Garza nodded to Colt as he entered the interview room, but when he saw Caitlyn, he swept his hair back and smiled. He held his hands out to take hers. "Caitlyn Reed. Thank you for coming."

"Mr. Garza," she responded without inflection.

"Tito. Please." He sat stiffly in the chair opposite her. "I know we're not friends, but I felt like you understood me that sad day in Moose Creek."

"I'll do my best to help you, Mr... Tito. But you have to help us first."

"You know they'll kill me if I talk. Don't you?"

Caitlyn leaned forward, folding her hands on the table. "I know they'll try. But we can protect you."

Garza sat back in his chair and considered her. They stared at each other for a long time. "You have to get me out of this place. I've already received one beating." He lifted his orange top, and Colt frowned at the man's bruised ribcage. "This was a warning."

Colt pushed back his chair and stood. "I'll talk to the chief about moving you to an isolated cell—if your information proves to be helpful."

Staring at Caitlyn, Garza continued. "I feel like I can trust you. You're the only one I believe will do what you say."

Caitlyn tilted her head. "I won't make you promises I can't keep."

"What kind of guarantee can you give me that I'll be protected after I testify?" He glanced up at Colt. "An isolated cell won't protect me from the guards on Trova's payroll."

"We can place you in a federal facility," Caitlyn offered.

"I don't think you appreciate Trova's reach. I can't be held in *any* type of jail facility. Don't you people have safe houses or something?"

Caitlyn rested back in her chair and narrowed her eyes at Garza. The man was handsome and charming, but Colt knew neither of those features fooled Caitlyn. Tito Garza was a wife-beating, drug-pushing thug, and neither of them felt any sympathy for him at all. But they needed his testimony. Garza obviously thought Caitlyn was a pushover. No doubt, that's why he requested her to be in this interview, but Colt figured she'd use that to her advantage.

"Yes, we do," she answered. "But, Tito, there's no way I'm going to be able to convince my boss to let us take you to one of those, unless the information you give us is rock-solid. It has to be enough to put your cousin away, for good."

"I've got what you need, but I have to be sure I'll be living my days out somewhere nice—like I'm used to. Where will the Marshals set me up in my new life? Maybe somewhere tropical? Do I have any choices?"

"Not a lot." Caitlyn gave him an apologetic smile. "But even if I knew, I couldn't tell you where you're going. That way you can't accidentally let the information slip to the wrong person."

"But my lifestyle will be like the one I'm accustomed to, right? I'll have an expense account or something?"

Colt willed himself not to laugh in the man's face. "They don't have any details at this point. But the important thing is they'll keep you alive."

Ignoring Colt, Garza reached toward Caitlyn across the table. "Maybe you'll come visit me? I know I'll have to give up all my acquaintances, but you're a Deputy Marshal, so that shouldn't include you."

The day Caitlyn spent more than even five minutes thinking about this dirtbag, she'd be giving him more than he deserved. Colt interjected. "We'll have to see who your contact is. But for now, we need you to tell us everything you can about the Trova crime syndicate."

Caitlyn leaned forward. "And I personally want to

know where Ray Burroughs is hiding out." She smiled sweetly.

Garza gave her a smarmy grin, his swagger returning. "Burroughs is a chump. He's hiding out up in North Dakota. You got a pen?" Garza sat back. "Now, as far as the Trova family goes, I have the details of the work he asked me to do for him here in Montana. Everything is documented and stored in a safety deposit box at my bank. I can also tell you who Tony's Mexican connections are. I can give you a list of names of the guys who work for him in New York, but I've never been privy to any of the money details there."

"Names are a good start." Colt handed Garza a yellow legal pad and a pen. "What bank is your safety deposit box in?"

Garza proceeded to write down the address of Burroughs's hideout in North Dakota. As he wrote a list of names, Garza explained that he and Anthony Trova were first cousins on their mothers' sides. That they'd been close until Trova had Garza's wife killed. He told them he hadn't trusted Trova since then, and that he feared Trova was planning to have him killed too.

"How does Burroughs fit into all this?" Colt asked.

"Burroughs is a distant cousin to Trova. I don't know how, exactly. Third cousin twice removed or some crazy shit. But he's from Trova's dad's side. Burroughs and I aren't technically related, and I think Trova's planning to order Burroughs to snuff me out."

"Why would he do that? You've been loyal to him ever since your wife was killed."

"First of all, when you guys blew up the meth lab, that

seriously put the hurt on Trova's western operation, and he blamed all of that on me. He listens to whatever crap Burroughs feeds him, and Burroughs will say anything to save his own skin."

Colt gestured at the pad on the table. "Keep writing. Be sure to put down everything you've told us and include all the details you know about Trova's drug dealings here and in New York. We'll be back in a few minutes." Colt helped Caitlyn out of her chair, and they stepped out of the room.

Caitlyn's eyes were bright, and she tugged on his sleeve. "I'll call Dirk. Burroughs is a job for the US Marshals. I can hitch a ride up to North Dakota with him, and we'll bring that SOB in."

"You aren't cleared to return to duty, Catie. You're not ready. You haven't had any time to deal with what happened to you." Colt wasn't surprised that she wanted to get back to work, but she hadn't healed physically or emotionally from her last ordeal yet.

"Come on, Colt. We've both been chasing after Burroughs. I'm going." She dialed Dirk, and after putting the call on speaker, told him her plans.

"Absolutely not." Dirk barked over the phone. "You're sitting this one out, Reed, and that's an order. My team and I will handle this. I'll call up to the New York office and get them working on the Trova angle from there."

Caitlyn's jaw tightened, and she handed Colt's phone back to him. He clicked off the speaker. "Dirk, this is Colt. Good luck and keep us posted."

"I will. Listen, I know Caitlyn's pissed at me, but no way is she recovered enough to go on a mission."

"Roger that. Thanks, Dirk. Call us as soon as you get him."

SILENCE PREVAILED for the first half hour on their return drive to Wyoming. Finally, Colt broke the ice. "I know you're disappointed about not getting to go with Dirk to North Dakota."

"I could have helped." She was angry, and her jaw hurt from clenching, but Dirk and Colt were right. She just didn't want to admit it. Didn't want to remember the terror of her abduction.

"Catie," Colt's fingers tightened on the steering wheel, and she turned to face him. "I thought I might never see you again last week. Knowing Payne had you, and knowing his MO. God, I was so scared." He stared straight ahead, most likely reliving his fear.

"I'm okay, Colt." She reached for his arm and pulled his hand from the wheel and held it in her lap.

He glanced at her. "Thank, God." His Adam's apple bobbed up and down his throat. "Listen. I don't want to wait another day to get married. I want to start our life together, right now."

She squeezed his hand. "Me too. There was a moment when I thought I might not escape, and my greatest regret was not being your wife. How will we work all this out with Jace… and Allison? All that?"

"I don't care. We'll figure it out."

"What do we do about Dylan and McKenzie? Their

wedding is only a week away. I don't want to steal their thunder."

"We don't need any thunder. Let's just get Pastor Slinglough and your family together and say our vows..."

"Okay." A burst of bubbly energy had her sitting up. She bit her lower lip. "Let's do it! How about tomorrow? No fuss."

Colt smiled at her then. "Perfect."

Caitlyn pulled out her phone and dialed. "Mom?"

30

"**W**hat are you going to wear?" McKenzie asked as she bounced on her toes in excitement.

Caitlyn laughed at her. "I don't know. I'm sure I have something that will work. It's not like we're planning the social event of the season. No one cares what I'll be wearing. The point is for Colt and me to say our vows and I dos. We don't care about clothes or any of that."

"Come on, Caitlyn. You have to dress for the occasion. Maybe you could wear your mom's wedding gown?"

"Are you kidding me? No way. Have you seen her dress?" Caitlyn laughed and rolled her eyes. "It looks like Little House on the Prairie married Gone With The Wind. Can you see me wearing a high-necked lace collar and a hoop skirt?"

"No. I can't." McKenzie opened Caitlyn's closet and stood before it, staring at the rack of western blouses and jeans. A clear plastic bag covered something tucked in the back corner. She pushed things aside and pulled out the yellow dress Caitlyn wore to her academy graduation party. "This! This dress is perfect!"

Caitlyn peeked over McKenzie's shoulder. "Oh yeah! I forgot I had that. Good idea. Colt loves that dress." She reached for the dress and tore away the thin plastic cover. Holding it up to her body, she gazed at herself in the mirror. Her excitement cooled as she noticed McKenzie watching her. "Hey, you're being a great sport about all this, by the way. Are you sure you don't mind us getting married so close to your wedding day? We could always elope."

McKenzie came up behind her and gave her a hug. Resting her chin on Caitlyn's shoulder, she spoke to her reflection. "Of course, I don't mind. You and Colt have been a long time coming. Besides, Dylan and I are still having the big white wedding I've dreamed of."

Caitlyn squeezed McKenzie's hands. "You're so sweet, and I'm beyond happy you're going to be my sister."

"Me too! I've always wanted a sister." McKenzie kissed her cheek and turned toward the door. "Want a beer?"

"Please." Caitlyn hung the dress from the top of her door and limped behind her friend to the kitchen. "Colt and I are planning to fly to Cancun for our honeymoon, but I'll be back in time for your bachelorette party. I made reservations at a B and B in Rapid City. I thought you, Addison, Stephanie, and I could party the first night and then spend the next day recovering at a spa. Mani-pedis, massages—the works. What do you think?"

"That sounds fantastic. I wish I had time to do something like that for you."

"I don't mind, honestly, Kenze. Besides, I don't want to

waste another day apart from Colt. Last week when Payne had me chained up... I was so scared..." Caitlyn let her words trail off. She'd successfully avoided the memories of her abduction until that moment. She swallowed hard. When she noticed her hands were trembling, her gaze flew to McKenzie.

"Oh, sweetie," McKenzie rushed to her and opened her arms. Caitlyn fell into her friend's embrace. "Hush, now. Of course, you were scared. But you're home now. Safe. You survived."

Images bombarded Caitlyn's mind. A raised belt. A striking rattlesnake. Her hand covered in thick, hot, almost-black blood. Bile rose in her throat, and she broke away from McKenzie's arms and stumbled to the toilet. Her body did its best to rid her of the terrifying experiences. She threw up until all she had left were dry heaves. Tears streamed over her cheeks, and she wiped her mouth with the back of her hand.

McKenzie pressed a cool cloth to her forehead and blotted her cheeks. "Do you want me to call Colt? Or Blake, maybe?"

"No. I'm fine now." She wasn't sure that she spoke the truth, but she didn't want Colt to know she was so badly shaken and calling Blake would be even worse. He'd want to run her through a bunch of medical and psychological tests. *No way.* "I'm fine. I think I just need a glass of water."

"Let me call Colt," McKenzie said on her way to get Caitlyn her water.

"No, please don't. He'll only worry." Caitlyn washed her face and brushed her teeth before sipping slowly from the glass of water. "I just need a little time. There's a lot going on."

"Maybe you two should wait to get married, after all."

"No!" Caitlyn's pulse spiked, and she slowed her breathing to control it. "No. Marrying Colt and getting away for a few days is exactly what I need." Her phone buzzed, and she crossed to the counter to see who was calling. "Hi, Pastor Slinglough."

"Hello Caitlyn. I got your message, and I would love to officiate at your wedding. I'm pleased to hear that you and Colt are getting married."

"Thank you. We're so happy you can do the honors."

"There's just one small problem. I'm out of town for a funeral, and I won't be back to Moose Creek for two days."

"Oh." Caitlyn dropped onto the couch. "I see. Okay. Let's plan the wedding for two days from now, then."

"If that works for you, I'll be there."

Caitlyn hung up the phone and leaned her head back against the cushion. "That throws a wrench in the works. We can't say our vows for two more days."

"I'm sorry." McKenzie sat next to her and held her hand. "Maybe you can use the extra time to rest. With any luck you'll be able to walk down the aisle without a crutch."

"Yeah, but this pushes our whole timeline back. Colt and I won't have time to go to

Cancun and get back in time for your wedding festivities."

"Maybe you can go on the trip after Dylan's and my ceremony."

"Maybe. Or, we could just drive up to the hunting cabin for a few days." Caitlyn picked up her phone and called Colt.

COLT HANDED Dylan a bottle of beer and sat next to him on the couch. "Who do you think will go to the series this year?"

They batted around their thoughts of who merited a chance and who should win the whole show before they grilled a pack of spicy bratwurst and settled in to watch the game.

Dylan tore open a bag of potato chips. "The girls are over at Caitlyn's tonight, making plans for your impromptu wedding ceremony. If I didn't know any better, I'd wonder why you two are suddenly in such a rush. No shotguns are pointed at you, are they?"

Colt laughed. "No. It's just that we've already wasted too much time, and with the events of the past week, we don't want to wait any longer. It's time to make it official."

"Where are you guys going to live? Here or Caitlyn's?"

"You know, we've never come to a decision about that." Colt took a juicy bite of his sausage and swallowed before he continued. "Catie obviously doesn't want to give up her place, but neither do I. This house is all I have left of my parents, and it's so convenient to work."

"Neither place is big enough for a family."

Colt nodded. "That's true. We'll need a second bedroom for Jace, no matter where we decide to live."

Dylan drained his beer before he asked, "How are you

doing with all that? We haven't had a chance to talk since you found out you had a son."

"Most days I'm still trying to get my head around it. He's a great kid, so that part is easy."

"How's Caitlyn dealing with it?" Dylan went to the fridge for a second beer. "Want one?"

"Sure." Colt kicked off his boots and propped his feet on the coffee table. "She's supportive, but I don't think she's happy about it. The thing is, I can't change the situation."

"You guys want to have kids of your own too, don't you?"

"Yeah. Eventually."

"So, Caitlyn's place makes the most sense then. There's room out there to build and add on."

"Good point. I guess I could sell this place and use the money for construction."

"I'll help when I can, and I bet my dad will, too. In fact, getting him out of my mom's hair would be a good thing these days."

"McKenzie mentioned things were a little rough between them lately. That's hard for me to imagine. They've always been so solid."

"Back when they had a common goal, they were. But now, my dad's retired and my mom wants to travel. I'm hoping when Kenze moves in, she'll be a buffer between them."

"Or maybe they need to figure out a new common goal."

Dylan smirked, "Yeah, like grandkids."

They tapped their bottles together and leaned back to

focus on the game. When Colt got up to get another bratz, his phone buzzed. He swiped to answer. "Hey, beautiful. How're the plans coming?"

Caitlyn groaned. "Well, I just talked to the pastor, and he's out of town for a couple of days. So, we'll have to wait until he gets back for our ceremony."

"A couple of days is okay. We've waited this long." He said the words casually, but his chest was heavy with disappointment.

"I know, but that cuts our trip plans short, too. I wondered what you'd think about just disappearing up to the hunting cabin for a few days. We could take Ren, and the horses, and just enjoy being away in nature."

"I love that idea. We can postpone the trip to Cancun till spring. I hear it's nicer that time of year, anyway."

"Good. That way, we will be back in time to do all the wedding events for McKenzie and Dylan." She paused. "Be sure to tell Allison we moved up our wedding date and that we'll be out of town for a few days on our honeymoon."

31

The following evening, Colt picked Caitlyn and Renegade up after he got off work, and they drove out to her parents' ranch for dinner. "I hope Dirk can get my truck back here this weekend. I hate not having a vehicle—even a torn-up one." She reached into the back seat to pat the culprit of her destroyed truck interior on his furry shoulder. Turning back to Colt, she asked, "Did you have a chance to talk to Allison today?"

Colt's shoulders slumped. "Yeah, but we didn't come to any agreement. I think we're going to have to use a mediator. We need to figure out how we want to handle the parenting schedule for Jace and agree on child support. I'm still hoping to avoid having to get an attorney."

Caitlyn bit down on the corner of her lip and glanced at him. "You probably should though, you know? I mean, whatever you two agree upon still needs to go through the court and be official. Just in case."

"Just in case, what?"

"What if you agree on a plan and then Allison decides to change it, or to move, or whatever? I think you need to protect yourself, legally."

Colt sighed and the muscles of his jaw flexed. Her phone buzzed, flashing Dirk's face on her screen. "Hey, Sterling. I was just talking about you. Do you think you'll be able to get my truck down here this weekend?"

"I'm not sure that's going to happen. Sorry, kid. But I am calling with good news. We surveilled the address Garza gave you for Burroughs, and sure enough, he was there. He was holed up in a double-wide on some acreage that would have been a nice spot if it wasn't littered with junk. We breached and apprehended him with no incident, which was nice for a change. He was just sitting in the living room watching TV with nothing on but his underwear. Made checking him for weapons an easy task." Dirk chuckled. "Now we have to transport him down to Denver to face his first charges. The Denver DA will bring him up on bank robbery and first-degree murder charges before sending him to stand trial in Utah for the jewelry store robbery and more murder charges."

"Then he'll come to Wyoming?"

"Yes, where they'll try him for kidnapping and murder. Colorado doesn't have the death penalty, but both Utah and Wyoming do. So, we'll see how he fairs."

"I imagine he never thought he'd get caught. Or that he believed his friends, or a cousin, in this case, was in a high enough position to make him untouchable."

"Who knows? But we'll be driving through Wyoming

this evening on our way down to Denver, and I thought maybe I could swing by. The convoy hauling Burroughs will keep going, but I wanted to check in on you. Then I'll catch up to them in Cheyenne later."

"Sure, we'd love to see you. We'll be at my family's ranch, though. You'll probably make it in time for dessert."

"Sounds good. See you soon. Stay out of trouble 'til then, will you?"

"Yeah, yeah." Caitlyn grinned as she ended the call. "That was Dirk. They caught Burroughs and are transporting him down to Denver tonight. I wish I could go with them."

Colt side-eyed her. "Seriously? You're still hobbling around on that ankle. Not to mention, we're getting married in two days."

"I know. I just wish I could see Burroughs get tossed into a cell. There's so much he needs to pay for."

"That's true, but he doesn't deserve any more of your time or energy. He'll get what he deserves, so let it go. By the way, have you made your first appointment with the psychologist?"

"Not yet. I'm waiting till after the weddings."

The minute they arrived at the ranch, Caitlyn sensed the tension between her mom and dad, though they both were cordial and polite to each other. In fact, it was the hyper display of manners that was out of place. She glanced at Dylan, who shook his head.

Caitlyn pushed through the awkwardness by telling her parents that she and Colt would say their vows in two days when the pastor returned home and that they were going to go up to the hunting cabin for a couple of days afterward. "I want to take a couple of horses up with us, but I still haven't got my truck back, and I don't trust Colt's Jeep to haul them."

Her dad shrugged. "You can borrow my truck for a few days. I'm not planning to go anywhere." Her mom made a scoffing sound.

"That'd be great. Thanks, Dad!" Caitlyn gave him a hug and pecked his cheek.

"So, Ma," her brother's voice held a false brightness. "Are we eating inside or out?"

"Ask your father what *he* wants to do." Caitlyn's mother pushed through the swinging door and went into the kitchen.

Caitlyn followed her and found her intently stirring a pot on the stove. "Mom?" She leaned against the counter next to her. "What's going on? Are you and Dad still fighting?"

"We're not fighting, Caitlyn."

"Okay. Are you still *not* fighting, then? What's going on? And don't say, 'Nothing,' because everyone here can feel it."

Her mom set her spoon on a plate next to the stove, and turning to Caitlyn, she crossed her arms over her chest. "It's a new phase of life for us, and we don't agree on how we want to live it. That's all."

"What do *you* want?"

"To live. To go on adventures—see the world. I think you, of all people, might understand how I feel. I can't imagine *you* wanting to sit around doing nothing besides waiting on Colt for the rest of your life."

"Damn straight. So, Dad doesn't want to travel or have any adventures, is that it?"

Her mom closed her eyes briefly before answering. "He wants to rest. I mean, I understand that he's worked hard his whole life, and he's looking forward to having a break, but so have I. He sees himself doing a lot of reading and fishing and then coming back here to a clean house and a home-cooked meal. But then my life doesn't change at all. I'd like a retirement too. I want a change from all the work I do, too, but your father refuses to understand that."

Caitlyn slid her arm around her mother's shoulders. "I'm sorry, Mom. I mean, I can see both sides of this issue, but what he wants isn't fair to you. Maybe you could travel somewhere with a friend? You'd get to have fun, and Dad would get to see how it is around here without all that you do."

"Maybe, but I don't know anyone who would want to go to Europe for a month with me."

"Go on your own, then."

Her mom looked startled. "I could never do that."

"Why not? You could sign up for a tour. Then you wouldn't be completely on your own. You might meet some new friends. At least look into it."

"You know, I think I will. I never thought of that, but I bet there are tours that go all around Europe, and then I could finish my trip in Ireland for a week or so. I'd love to see where my family came from."

"There you go. Good for you."

"But, what about your dad? How do you think he'll react when I tell him this idea?"

"He'll grumble about it, but just remind him that he's welcome to come along if he wants to. Besides, when Dylan and McKenzie get back from their honeymoon, they can keep an eye on him."

Caitlyn's mom cupped her face. "Don't ever lose your ability to see things so clearly and your determination to follow your dreams. I wish I was more like you in that way."

"You are, Mom. You just lost your voice along the way because you always put everyone else first."

"I guess that's what moms do." Her mom kissed her cheek. "Now, go tell everyone dinner will be ready in about ten minutes. Let's eat outside on the picnic table tonight." She beamed with renewed energy.

Caitlyn went to do as her mom asked but was unsettled by her comment about being a mom. Caitlyn couldn't help but wonder if she had it in her to be so self-sacrificing. Guilt pressed against her conscience when she thought about Jace. Would she ever be rid of the discomfort she felt with his presence in their lives? Colt was already in a place where he thought about how his decisions would affect his son. But she didn't want to have to scale back her life in consideration of someone else's kid —and that made her feel like a selfish jerk. On the other hand, she didn't want to be sixty and look back on her life and feel like she'd missed out on her dreams just so someone else could live theirs. Why did life have to be so difficult?

After everyone helped carry their plates, glasses, and silverware outside, Caitlyn plugged in the twinkle lights that were strung in the tree overhead. "This is nice. Good idea to eat out here, Mom."

Dylan and McKenzie sat across the table from Colt and her, and her parents sat in chairs on the opposite ends. The conversation seemed forced, a little too bright. Everyone did their best to keep the mood elevated until her mom set down her silverware and folded her napkin, placing it on her plate.

"John, I've decided to go on a European tour after Dylan and McKenzie's wedding. I'll book the first one available. I'd like you to go with me if you want to, but I understand if you choose not to."

Silence fell around the table, and all eyes shifted to her dad. His gaze narrowed, and he placed his steak knife across the top of his plate. Lifting his napkin, he wiped his mouth, and then pushed his chair backward. "I'm sure you'll have a wonderful time... by yourself." He left the table and went inside the house.

Four heads swiveled back to her mom, who looked as though she might cry. Caitlyn reached for her hand. "Good for you, Mom. Stick to your guns."

Dylan threw down his napkin. "Don't you think you should stay out of it, Caitlyn? This is between Mom and Dad."

"No, I *don't* think I should stay out of it. Someone needs to support Mom. I suppose you think she should just keep working her ass off around here, too. When does *she* get a break? You guys just love having someone slave around the house for you, don't you? How do you feel about that, McKenzie? You're next in line."

McKenzie raised her hands in surrender. "I'm staying

out of this. It's not my place to say anything, one way or another."

Colt picked up his and Caitlyn's plates. "Me either. But I'll be glad to do the dishes tonight. Thanks for dinner, Stella." Colt made a hasty exit, and McKenzie followed him.

Dylan swung his leg over the bench and sat facing their mom. "I don't think you should keep working so hard, Mom. I get where you're coming from, too. But you and Dad have never wanted us to butt into your disagreements. That's all I was trying to say."

"You're right, but now that you're adults, I guess I look at you more like friends than children. So, I talked to Caitlyn about it, and I'm going to pursue my dreams. I'll only be gone a month. It's not like I'm leaving forever."

Tires crunched on the gravel, and Caitlyn craned her neck to see if maybe her dad was leaving, but his truck remained parked. A black SUV with its headlights turned off edged its hood around the corner. Caitlyn reached for her sidearm and maneuvered herself between her mother and the strange vehicle.

Suddenly, the headlights flashed on along with the hazard blinkers. Flood lights around the house blazed on at the same time and Caitlyn scanned the scene. What the hell was going on?

The driver's door of the SUV opened, and Dirk Sterling got out. Caitlyn lowered her weapon and re-holstered it. "What are you doing, Dirk? I could have shot you."

"No, you wouldn't. Your trigger discipline is too good." He laughed. "I brought you a present."

"What? Do you have Burroughs in there?" Caitlyn went to the gate and tried to see in through the tinted windows.

"No. Although, he deserves to have to sit in a kennel all the way to Denver."

"What?" He wasn't making any sense. Caitlyn's gaze darted to the back kitchen door. Colt and McKenzie had come back out, and Colt had a goofy grin plastered to his face. "What's going on?"

Dirk opened the passenger's door. "Come see."

Confused, Caitlyn opened the gate and walked toward Dirk's car. "Who's in there?"

"No one. But I think Renegade will like this new space. Don't you?"

Caitlyn crunched her brows together. What was Dirk talking about? She bent to look inside the SUV. Then abruptly stood straight up. "Really? This is for me? For me, and Ren?"

"It sure is." Dirk's dark eyes sparkled, and he gave her a rare grin. "When I explained to Marshal Williams that your abduction would never have happened if you had a fully functioning K9 vehicle outfitted with a door-pop mechanism, she got busy locating one right away."

"Is this why it was taking you so long to bring me my truck?"

"Yep." His dark eyes shimmered.

Caitlyn reached up and hugged her stoic partner, and Dirk chuckled. "It's the least the USMS can do for you and Renegade, and it's high time."

"Thank you, Dirk. And thanks for driving it down here." Caitlyn whistled. "Come on Ren! Check out your new digs! This is just like Logan's FBI K9 vehicle." Renegade leapt into the kennel and sniffed all around while Caitlyn slid into the driver's seat. "Look! It has a built-in computer and everything."

"And an automatic temperature gauge that keeps it cool enough for Renegade at all times. You can connect the controls to your phone, so you can keep an eye on the car even if you're inside. I don't think we'll have it painted. It's better when we can go in un-marked."

Colt approached the car and leaned in. "This is awesome. Thanks, Dirk. I know I'll feel better knowing that Catie can remotely open Renegade's door if she needs help."

"Yeah, it's too bad you didn't have it the day Payne attacked you, Reed. But I sure am proud of the way you handled yourself." He pointed out more features. "See, Ren can stick his head through this space, and you can still pet him while you're driving. There is only room for one bad guy, though."

Caitlyn laughed. "How would you like to be *that* guy, riding all the way to the police department with an angry K9 breathing through the slats at you?"

"There's a compartment behind the kennel to store all your gear. I think you're gonna love this ride." Dirk opened the back hatch for everyone to see.

John wandered out from the house, holding up his cell phone. "Logan wants to see your new vehicle, too." He aimed the screen at Caitlyn, and she squealed.

"Did you know about this, Log?"

Her middle brother beamed at her from FaceTime. "I

did! Marshal Williams called me for a consult, so I did my best to get you all the bells and whistles."

"Thank you!"

"You and Renegade, both deserve it. Now, go take it for a spin. I'll see you soon." Logan signed off, and Caitlyn peered out from the driver's seat.

"Who wants the first ride?"

32

Two long days later, Colt stood with Renegade, Dylan, and Logan, at the edge of Moose Lake's crystalline blue water. The gentle waves lapping the shore were the only music playing as the love of his life walked down the narrow beach toward him. He strained against the fabric of the one suit he had in his closet. He didn't remember when he'd last worn it, but he'd grown since then. Caitlyn wore the yellow dress he loved, and it glowed gold in the evening sunset behind her, which also rimmed her long, loose curls in a fiery halo. She looked like some divine ethereal creature floating toward him, her limp barely noticeable. She carried a bouquet of wildflowers gathered from the high meadow above the ranch. Their eyes met and held. His heart clogged his throat. Colt had longed for this moment for over a decade, and it was finally here.

Everyone who mattered was there. Except for Jace. Even Logan and Addison had flown up for the weekend. But earlier, when he'd asked Allison if Jace could come, she'd been difficult, claiming it was *her* parenting day, not his. Colt was disappointed, but he wouldn't let anything ruin this perfect day.

John escorted his daughter toward Colt, and she paused to kiss her dad's cheek when he released Caitlyn to Colt's arm. She'd always been the most beautiful woman in the world to him, but tonight he couldn't take his eyes off of her. She grinned up at him. *Love you,* she mouthed. Renegade's tail swept a wedge in the dirt as he sat looking up at his people.

They held hands and spoke vows from their hearts before exchanging rings. Pastor Slinglough finally told Colt he could kiss his bride, and his whole life opened before him in the single best second of his life. They turned to greet their family as a newly married couple, and Colt's mouth dropped open. At the back of the gathering, Allison stood with Jace, dressed in a little man's suit. His son held a single yellow rose and looked impossibly young and unsure. Allison gave him a little nudge.

Caitlyn's family quieted as the boy walked past them. He handed Caitlyn the flower. "Congratulations," he said and stepped back.

Colt gripped Jace's shoulder, and his son leaned in and slid his thin arms around Colt's waist. Tears sprang to his eyes, and he returned the hug, pulling Caitlyn into it with him. How strange and unexpected all of this was, but how wonderful, too. He looked up and nodded at Allison before he spoke to Jace. "I'm so glad you're here."

"My mom wasn't going to let me, but then Caitlyn called." He grinned up at her. "My mom *never* changes her mind. I don't know what you said, but whatever it was, worked."

Caitlyn laughed and touched his cheek. "I just said that our family needed to be here, and that included you."

Colt figured there was more to the conversation than that, and he loved Caitlyn even more in that moment, if that were possible.

In seconds, the Reed family surrounded them, offering hugs and handshakes of congratulations. Allison stood off to the side, looking out of place and like she wished she was anywhere else.

Caitlyn smiled up at him and followed his gaze to Jace's mom. "Come with me." She took Colt's hand and tugged him toward Allison. "Thanks for bringing Jace, today. I hope you'll come back to the house for dinner."

Allison was taken aback. "I couldn't, possibly."

"Of course, you can. You're family too, after all. I'd love it for Jace if we all got along. Wouldn't you?"

Colt's heart pounded against his chest wall as he waited for Allison's response.

"I would too. But are you sure, Caitlyn? I'd understand if you didn't want me there. This is your day."

"I do want you there. I think this is the best way to start this next chapter of our lives. We need to be comfortable around each other and the better friends we can be, the better it will be for Jace. Don't you agree?"

Allison's eyes grew moist, and she bobbed her head. Caitlyn gave her a quick hug. "Good, then it's settled. Do you know how to get my parents' house?"

"I can follow everyone."

Jace ran up to them. "Mom! Can I ride in Caitlyn's cool

new dog car? Colt said if you say it's okay, I can ride in the prisoner's seat!"

Allison blinked at her son. "What?"

Colt laughingly explained how the K9 vehicle was set up, and Allison agreed to let Jace ride in the new Explorer next to Renegade.

After all the congratulations were said, Stella shepherded everyone to their cars. "Back to the house for dinner, everyone." Stella walked Caitlyn to her car and kissed her cheek. "I couldn't be happier for you two." She watched Jace climb into the single back seat. "For you *three*," she amended. "Now let's enjoy your wedding supper together before you and Colt run off on your honeymoon."

Caitlyn's mom had arranged a bountiful spread for them back at the ranch house. John grilled T-bones on the barbeque while Dylan and McKenzie carried the prepared feast to the elegantly set table. Candles glowed from the midst of a sunflower garland draped down the center.

"Mom, it's beautiful. I can't believe you pulled all this together at the last minute." Caitlyn reached for her mother's hands and kissed her cheek.

"Addison and McKenzie gave me plenty of help." Stella's gaze panned her family, and a warm smile graced her face. "I'm so happy for you and Colt."

After filling themselves to the brim with steak, creamy mashed potatoes, grilled vegetables, and home-baked bread, Caitlyn and Colt were ready to cut their wedding cake. There was no white buttercream frosting for them. Instead, the newlywed's cake was Caitlyn's favorite Death By Chocolate Cake.

Though all the guests ate their fill, there was still a ton of food left at the end of the evening. So, Caitlyn's mom packed them a hamper filled with leftovers and half of the cake. "This should keep you from starving for at least one day."

"Thanks, Mom. It's much better than the PBJs *I* was planning on."

Her mom pursed her lips. "You think you've got everyone fooled, but I saw all the delicious food you packed in the cooler. PBJs indeed."

Caitlyn shrugged and giggled. "Well, I have to keep Colt's strength up."

Her mom swatted her arm with a dish towel. "Go on, now. You two have a wonderful time. I think Dylan and Logan got the trailer hooked up to your dad's truck and loaded the horses. You should be all set."

"Thanks for everything, Mom. Really. You helped make today even more special."

AFTER SAYING THEIR GOODBYES, Caitlyn and Colt were on their way to the Reeds' hunting cabin high up in the Big Horn Mountains. They had four days of nothing to do but enjoy each other. Her idea of the best kind of honeymoon possible. "You know, I'm glad we had to cancel our trip to Cancun. I think spending this time together, just you, me, and Renegade with no other people around, will be perfect."

Colt took her hand and kissed it before resting it on his leg as they drove into the night. Her phone rang, and Dirk's face filled her screen. Smiling at Colt, she sent the call to voicemail. But he rang again. "What's up, Dirk? This better be important." Colt side-eyed her and raised his eyebrow. She held up her finger, asking for one second.

"I'm back up here in North Dakota. Burroughs gave his guards the slip when they stopped to use the facilities at a visitor's center. Just wanted to let you know he's back in the wind."

"What?" Caitlyn sat up and pressed the phone tighter against her ear. "How could they let that happen?"

"Apparently, he overtook the guard that went into the men's room with him and got ahold of the officer's gun. Burroughs knocked him out and cuffed the guy to the sink. Next, he surprised the second guard in the lobby. After taking his weapon too, Burroughs used the cop's cuffs to lock him to a display counter. Burroughs escaped out the back and it was twenty or more minutes before the cops waiting in the parking lot went inside to check on their partners."

Caitlyn's stomach balled up and she swallowed hard. "I can't believe it."

"I know, but don't worry, we'll find him. And when we do, we have all we need to put him away for the rest of his life—*if* he manages to escape the death penalty. A team of Marshals in New York has Trova under surveillance and plans to move on him soon. I know you just got hitched, but I wondered if you want to help us track down Burroughs. It would sure help to have a K9."

Caitlyn smiled at Colt. "Not a chance. I still need to be cleared both physically and psychologically for duty, but besides that, Colt and I just got married and we're on our way to our honeymoon. But… you can be sure I'll call you as soon as we get back."

***

Thank you for reading BLOODLINE.

I HOPE you enjoyed the thrill of riding along with Caitlyn as she made her desperate escape, and with Colt and Renegade, who raced to find her! The next book in the series continues their story and their fight for Justice, Integrity, and Service with the US Marshals Service.

NEXT BOOK IN THE SERIES:

TRIFECTA

Book 6 in the Tin Star K9 Series

The fast-paced, action-packed career of the US Marshal's rising star K9 team—Deputy Marshal Caitlyn Reed and her dog, Renegade—turns toward the tranquil rolling hills of Tennessee, when Caitlyn is assigned to oversee a racehorse barn recently seized by the Marshals Service. The job seems like vacation duty until several high-dollar horses go missing, shots are fired, and Renegade's life hangs in the balance.

Caitlyn's new husband, Sheriff Colt Branson, is back at home in Wyoming assimilating to his new role as a father and tending to the seemingly mundane duties of a small-town sheriff. But things heat up when cattle on several ranches along the creek mysteriously die, and a simple traffic stop turns deadly.

When Caitlyn chases the horse thieves into the seedy underbelly of the racing world, she tracks the roots of corruption all the way to the streets of New York City. In Moose Creek, Colt uncovers a surprising connection to Caitlyn's case. The question remains, will they all survive the unravelling of this twisted conspiracy, or will darkness ultimately prevail?

Join the Posse to find out!

Order TRIFECTA today!

IF YOU ENJOYED READING Bloodline ~ Book 5 in the Tin Star K9 Series, I would be most honored if you would please write a quick review.

Review Bloodline
Thank you!

FOR FREE BOOKS and to join my reader group, please visit my website at Jodi-Burnett.com

ALSO BY JODI BURNETT

Flint River Series

Run For The Hills

Hidden In The Hills

Danger In The Hills

A Flint River Christmas (Free Epilogue)

A Flint River Cookbook (Free Book)

FBI-K9 Thriller Series

Baxter K9 Hero (Free Prequel)

Avenging Adam

Body Count

Concealed Cargo

Mile High Mayhem

Tin Star K9 Series

RENEGADE

MAVERICK

CARNIVAL (Novella)

MARSHAL

JUSTICE

BLOODLINE

TRIFECTA

ACKNOWLEDGMENTS

First, as always, I thank God for blessing me with both the inspiration and the ability to write. Without Him, I can do nothing.

So many people pitch in to get a book launched and I'm grateful for so many folks. During the writing of this book, I had the amazing opportunity to attend the Writer's Police Academy in Green Bay, Wisconsin. The trainers at the academy were amazing professionals and I learned notebooks full of information, much of which shows up here and there throughout this book.

I also had a fascinating interview with my rural county's sheriff, Tim Norton, who had over twenty years of police K9 experience in Phoenix, AZ, before coming to Colorado to be our local sheriff. He is starting up a K9 unit here in Elbert County and has one dog, Rico, so far. Everything in their K9 unit is acquired through donation. So, I held a fundraiser to help them get a training bite suit and many of my wonderful and generous readers pitched in to make that happen! I have the best readers in the world!

I've had many friends and family members encourage me through the writing of this book, along with my incredible beta readers who help me find any holes that need filling. I'm beyond grateful to you all. And of course, my greatest appreciation goes to my husband who somehow knows when to encourage, when to push, when to walk away without stirring me up when I'm frustrated at the words. He sees it all, the good, the bad, and the ugly, and still hangs around to encourage me. Thank you, Chris. You are the best! (It's why I married you!) I love you!

Thank you to all my readers. You are the ones who complete my work. Without readers, books are merely objects to gather dust. Readers make the stories inside come to life. You are the magic dust over it all. Thank you!

ABOUT THE AUTHOR

Jodi Burnett loves writing suspense thrillers with a spark of romance from her small ranch in Colorado. She is the author of the Flint River Series and the FBI-K9 Series. In addition to writing stories and enjoying in the country with her horses and dogs, Jodi fosters her creative side by watercolor painting, quilting, and stained glass. She is a member of Sisters In Crime, and Novelists Inc.

facebook.com/JodiBurnettAuthor
twitter.com/jodi_writes
instagram.com/jodiburnettauthor